# WARRIOR
## ON THE
# MOUND

## SANDRA W. HEADEN

HOLIDAY HOUSE · NEW YORK

HOLIDAY HOUSE is registered in the U.S. Patent and Trademark Office.

Printed and bound in December 2023 at Maple Press, York, PA, USA.

www.holidayhouse.com

First Edition

1 3 5 7 9 10 8 6 4 2

Library of Congress Cataloging-in-Publication Data is available.

ISBN: 978-0-8234-53788 (hardcover)

# DEDICATION TK

# Chapter 1
## POPLAR FIELD
*March 1939*

In a few hours, me and my boys, the Pender County Rangers, are gonna do something we ought not to.

We'll skip school, sneak over the county line, and take a look at the new baseball field they built for the white boys in New Hanover County. If we stay on the back roads, no one will ever even know what we're up to.

Time was I could do a thing like this by myself, or talk my best friend, Mason, into going with me. But everything's different this year. Harder. I need all the Rangers to keep me strong.

Especially since today's my daddy's birthday and all. That's why we're going to see that fancy new baseball field. Every year I do something special for him. Most times, it's a small thing, like carving his initials in a wallet as a gift for him. But this year I'm taking Daddy Mo to Poplar Field, letting him see it through my eyes, 'cause that's the only way he can. He died when I was eight.

I reckon he was one of the best pitchers in the Negro Baseball Leagues. I aim to be just like him. Sometimes that's mighty hard!

Just like the floor of our pantry—that's pretty hard, too, especially when you've got to sleep on it. Having two quilts doesn't help much. Better ask Gran for another one.

There are shelves on both sides of me, stuffed with beans, rice, flour, and cornmeal, and if I stretch out my arms, I can touch them. That's how I know that my days sleeping in the pantry are numbered. My head almost touches the back wall, and pretty soon my feet will stick out so far they'll be under the kitchen table. (I haven't *always* slept in here. When I was younger, me and my sister, Hope, had a bed in the back of the house. But when I got a little bigger, Gran moved me out, first to the front room—which was too cold in winter—and then here. Yeah, it's cramped, but it's warm and snug.)

Lordy. I'm still sleepy. I yawn, pull a quilt up over my face to shut out the morning chill, and close my eyes. I know it's 'bout time to get up, but…

Something soft hits me in the face.

"Dang it, Hope!" I shoot up, a frown on my face. That girl threw my own dirty sock at me!

"Watch your mouth, Cato Jones!" Hope's grinning face pokes through the curtain in the pantry doorway. She's wearing a blue blouse with ruffles on the front, and a skirt with blue and white polka dots. Her hair is in two plaits with a blue ribbon on each one.

"You going to church?" I ask.

"No, silly! I'm all dressed up because Isaac might come home today. It *is* Daddy Mo's birthday."

That's not what Isaac wrote in his letter, and she knows it. He won't be home today, and we're not having the birthday dinner 'til he *does* get here.

Hope must have read my mind, because she shakes her finger at me. "Rev says if you want something bad enough, and you pray about it, it'll happen. That's how I know Isaac is going to be home today."

I shake my head. "Wake up, girl. If Gran thought Isaac was coming today, she would've been getting ready."

"She's cooking something, so I reckon she thinks he might."

"Gran is always cooking something."

Hope rolls her eyes at me, twisting the black ribbon on the locket she always wears around her neck. Inside that locket there's pictures of our mother, Clarise Hopewell Jones, who died birthing Hope, and our father, Moses Octavius Jones. Folks say we're the spitting image of them: Hope with thick black hair, cocoa-brown skin, and light brown eyes like Mama, me with Daddy Mo's high cheekbones and skin the color of the dark brown molasses that we both loved so much.

But I've got plenty growing to do if I'm gonna be six feet tall like he was. And plenty work to do if I'm gonna come close to pitching as good as him.

"Time to get up, Romeo," says Hope, batting her eyes. She's been teasing me ever since she heard me trying to sweet-talk my best friend Mason's cousin, Joann.

"Girl, leave me alone!" I grab the sock she threw from the pile of clothes next to me and throw it back at her. I only miss because she closes the curtain with a giggle.

"Mason's waiting for you on the porch. Why's he here so early?"

I don't answer her.

"What kind of trouble are you planning to get into this time?"

"Nun-a-yo beeswax!" I say. When she peeks through the curtain again, I throw another sock at her.

Hope narrows her eyes and stares at me, just like Gran. "You better watch out. One day you're gonna step in something even Papa Vee can't get you out of."

She disappears, leaving the curtain open just a bit. The smell of fatback frying on the stove drifts into the pantry. Hmm. I can almost taste it. I stretch, dress, and reach for my Rangers baseball cap on the bottom shelf. My hand brushes against the cap next to it, gray with black stripes, an *M* on the front for the Kansas City Monarchs. This was Daddy Mo's cap, from when he was in the Negro American League.

Four years.

That's how long my daddy's been gone. Will it ever stop hurting so much? I bite down hard on my lower lip to hold back the tears.

When I pick up the hat, Isaac's letter falls out. I read it again, letting my eyes rest on the last part:

Be home soon. Will miss Daddy Mo's birthday. Sorry.
Bringing a teammate. You'll like him.

3

I fold and stuff the paper into the blanket roll where I keep presents I've made for Daddy Mo over the years: a whistle, a bird I whittled, that sort of thing. Then I take off my Rangers cap and put Daddy Mo's cap on my head instead, pulling it down snug and tight. I grab my glove, shove it under my arm, and stuff a few baseballs into the front pockets of my pants.

"*Cato Jones!* Stop lazin' around and get up, boy!"

Gran's voice is sweet and sharp at the same time. I hear her feet scraping along the kitchen floor in Papa Vee's old shoes.

"Yes'm," I say.

I poke my head out of the curtain and stare at Gran, waiting for her to notice me, but she's focused on stirring something in a bowl on the table. Like Hope, she's all dressed up, wearing a spotless white apron and an ironed gray morning frock. The bright yellow kerchief that Daddy Mo bought her from Kansas City is tied in a knot above her forehead. The color of it makes her dark skin look extra brown.

"You going to church too?" I ask, grinning.

"Boy, you know I always dress up and bake a cake on Moses's birthday. And when Isaac gets home, I'll put on an even fancier dress—and make a feast, too."

"Is that Daddy Mo's favorite cake, chocolate with pecans on top?"

"This one's coconut. I'll save the chocolate cake for the birthday dinner." Gran cuts her eyes at me and smiles, showing her dimples. "And you'd better not lay a hand on this cake. I'm giving it to my healing sister, Mary Agnes."

"Yes'm. But don't blame me if you see a piece gone. The Devil loves coconut cake."

"Well, if the Devil comes by here, he'd better not look like a bushy-headed colored boy wearing Moses's baseball cap."

We both laugh. I lay my glove in a chair, walk over to the stove, and grab four hot biscuits out of the pan. I rip them in half and lay them out on the table, then grab the molasses jar, hold it high in the air, tilt it to the side, and move it around so the sweet goodness falls in circles on the bread.

"Boy, you know that's too much," says Gran, shaking her head.

"Hey, I'm growing," I say, standing a little taller.

Some fatback is in the cast-iron frying pan. I grab a fork, take four pieces, put one on each biscuit, and slap the tops on. Then I shove the biscuits into a paper sack, grab my glove, and head out the back door, kissing Gran on the cheek as I go. "Bye!"

Hope is sitting on the back steps holding something in her lap.

"Lordy. Another critter? What is it this time?"

Hope lifts a kitten up in the air. "This here is Moses. He showed up this morning. I'll bet it's Daddy Mo's spirit come to visit on his birthday."

The kitten's little head leans back in a yawn. Hope lowers him back onto her lap. He sinks into her and goes to sleep.

"So, what's the matter with it?" I say, leaning down for a closer look.

"Nothing."

"For real? Most of your critters are sick or near dead."

Hope ignores my comment and strokes the cat's back. Low purring sounds come out of it. "Mason's still on the front porch, you know. Waiting for you." She stops petting Moses. "Hey, how come you're wearing Daddy Mo's cap?"

"Nun-a-yo beeswax," I say, jumping off the back porch and onto the ground.

Papa Vee's in the yard, near the barn with his helpers, Nate and Ollie. They're loading the pickup truck for a trip to the fields to turn the soil for planting green beans, okra, and other things we'll eat all summer. I wave at them and keep walking toward the front.

"You late for school again, Cato?" asks Papa Vee.

"No suh!" I say, turning to face Papa Vee but walking backward all the while. "Me and Mason are gonna run all the way and slide into our seats before the bell rings."

Dang it! Told a lie. I know good and well I'm planning to skip.

Guiltily, I turn and run into the front yard, past Mason sitting on the front steps and down the dirt road leading toward the schoolhouse. Holding his catcher's mitt under his arm, Mason takes off after me and soon catches up. The front pockets of his pants bulge with baseballs, just like mine.

Finally out of sight, we quit running. "You got some biscuits for me?" pants Mason.

"Yeah," I say, taking my two-biscuit share and handing him the paper sack.

He looks inside. "Only two?"

"Hey, Isaac's coming home any day now. We have to save some for him."

"Uh-huh," says Mason, rolling his eyes at me. He bites down on a biscuit, says, "Hmm, fatback," then gobbles the rest of it. By now, I've eaten one biscuit too. We race to see who's first to finish their second one.

Not hard. I win.

"Why're you wearing Daddy Mo's cap?" Mason asks. I don't answer him, just take off running again 'cause it feels better than walking.

It's not long before Mason catches up with me. "Only a few weeks 'til the Rangers go to Raleigh. You ready?" He's a little winded. "Rev says we might get to watch the Newark Eagles practice—maybe even play a game with them!"

"Yeah. We're lucky they do their spring training in Carolina. You know, Miss Effa Manley might want to take me with them when she sees me pitch."

"What? Just because Daddy Mo was a great pitcher and now Isaac is too?" Mason gets real quiet for a while. Then he says, "There is something I've been wanting to ask you, though."

I laugh and slow my pace. "Hey, you're my best friend. You can ask me anything. Well... Uh, almost anything."

Mason looks at me sideways, then stares straight ahead. "Does it bother you? That players on other teams laugh when they see your windup? It's kinda... different... from anything Daddy Mo or Isaac ever did."

The muscles in my stomach tighten. Mason's never asked me anything like this before. I know it looks strange when I pitch—but it works. "Nah. Once we beat the snot out of them, it wipes the grins right off their faces. After a while, they know better."

The silence lasts only a few minutes before I say, "Why'd you ask me that?"

Mason shrugs. "I don't know. Just wondered if it hurt your feelings, what with you coming from a pitching family. That's all."

The moment feels tense. I mean, it's never a great feeling when somebody pokes fun at me.

"You still got your heart set on meeting Satchel Paige this summer?" asks Mason.

"Yeah, man!" I raise both arms up over my head and punch the air with my fists. "When Isaac comes home, I'm going back to Kansas City with him. Gonna meet all of the Kansas City Monarchs and get pitching lessons from Satchel Paige himself!"

"If you say so, Cato. I know him and Isaac are friends, but do you think he'll have time for you?" Mason's mouth curls up on one side.

"Sho'nuff," I insist.

After another half mile or so, we see our boys, the Pender County Rangers, sitting under our sycamore tree. They call our community Sycamore Grove 'cause so many like it grow around here. On one side of that tree is Pender County Normal School, and on the other is the baseball field. That's where we live most of our lives: Moses Fleetwood Walker Field, named for one of the first colored men to play with a Major League Baseball team. (Papa Vee says that was in the eighteen hundreds, before the "Gentleman's Agreement" said coloreds couldn't play on white teams. Huh. Those men don't sound like gentlemen to me.)

I look at Mason and I know we're thinking the same thing.

Laughing, we run right past our teammates and wave for them to follow. They all grab their gloves, stuff the baseballs they're carrying deeper into their pockets, scramble to their feet, and dash after us. School hasn't opened yet, so there's no one to see us cut.

"I reckon we'll be the first colored players from around here to lay eyes on Poplar Field!" Mason looks over his shoulder. We're still ahead of our teammates.

7

"Hey! That's how it's s'posed to be!" I say. "The Pender County Rangers are the best colored team in eastern Carolina. We should be the first to do everything!"

"Yeah!" me and Mason say at the same time.

When our teammates catch up, I turn to face them, running backward. "Double time, Rangers! We've still got a ways to go."

"Anybody got something to eat?" yells our shortstop, Skeeter.

"Criss-a-mighty!" says Mason, frowning. "Skeeter, you knew you'd get hungry. Why didn't you bring some food?"

"I brought something, but I ate it."

Mason rolls his eyes, digs into his back pocket, and hands Skeeter a piece of beef jerky.

"Thanks," says Skeeter. "Hey Cato, where's your Rangers cap?" Before I can answer him, he stuffs the jerky into his mouth, starts chewing, and asks, "Mason, you got any more?"

Lordy! I can tell Skeeter isn't the only one who's gonna want food before long. Breakfast doesn't last long at our age. I turn around to face the team. "Who else is 'bout to die from hong-ry?"

Nine hands shoot up in the air. That's everybody but me and Mason.

"Man! What's the matter with you fellas?" I shake my head. "You'll have to wait."

"But Blackburn's Store is just up ahead," says Mason.

I shoot a mean look at Mason, then bite down hard on the inside of my lip. Blackburn's Store? That name sends chills all through me.

Grown folks in Sycamore Grove whisper about the owner, Mr. Luke Blackburn, then hush up when young'uns try to listen. Thought I heard Rev say he did something bad to colored people. He even called him a devil one time. Whatever he did, I figure he might do it again.

Truth be told, I could live a long life and die happy if I never laid eyes on Mr. Luke Blackburn.

# Chapter 2
## SOUR PICKLES

The team is still talking about Blackburn's Store, and I'm getting knots in my stomach. Maybe it's 'cause of the look I see on Rev's face when he whispers Blackburn's name to Gran or Papa Vee. Maybe it's 'cause colored people in Sycamore Grove hardly ever go there. We'd rather walk the extra mile to Wilson's Store, where Mr. Dave and Miss Irene always have a kind word for us. (Best of all, they let the Rangers stand in the backyard and drink the sodas we buy, even when there's white ladies sitting on the porch or white men smoking cigars in the yard.)

Today, though, we've got no time to go to Wilson's Store, so I take in a deep breath and get ready to face Mr. Luke Blackburn.

"All right, fellas, me and Mason will go in and buy nabs and sodas for everybody," I announce, handing my glove to CP, our center fielder. We all know that a bunch of colored boys can't walk into a white man's store at the same time. "How many want peanut butter nabs?"

Five hands shoot up in the air. The rest will get cheese nabs.

"Who wants Co-cola?" asks Mason. Skeeter and his cousin, Raymond D., raise their hands. Then we count all that want orange, grape, and Pepsi-Cola.

I grab Mason's cap off his head and hold it out in front of me. "Drop your coins," I say.

"Hey!" Mason yells, but he doesn't reach for his cap.

When the last coin is dropped in, me and Mason finally cross the road to Blackburn's store.

It looks so different from Wilson's Store. These walls are sad and unpainted.The walls at Wilson's are a cheery white. And there's plenty of colored folks, coming and going, yelling "hey!" or throwing up a hand to wave.

Me and Mason walk up the creaky steps and stare at the closed wooden door.

"Is he open?" Mason looks at me, then back at the door.

"This time a morning, he ought to be." I slowly open the screen door and reach for the door latch.

Mason stretches his arm past me and knocks, loud and annoying. I shoot a mean look at him, but I open the door and go inside.

It's cool and dark in here. There are windows, but heavy blue curtains keep the light out. The brightness that we left outside makes it hard for us to see, so we stop and wait before creeping to the counter.

"Anybody here?" I put the cap full of coins down.

No one answers.

A jar of peppermint candies is right in front of us, so I open it, grab a handful, and lay them next to Mason's cap.

"Cato! Don't touch anything!" Mason whispers.

"He has to see what we want to buy," I shoot back.

Gingerly, I walk to the back of the store. It's even darker here, but I can make out some things. There's sacks leaning against the wall with the word BEANS on some and FLOUR on others. Empty boxes are stacked almost to the ceiling. Small barrels of molasses sit in a corner on top of one another. I walk over and lift the lid on one, smelling the thick, dark goodness. I'm tempted to stick a finger in, but I don't.

"Cato?" Mason calls out from the front of the store. "Man, what are you doing?"

"Looking for sodas," I say. "They've got to be back here somewhere."

Finally, I see a tin washtub filled with soda bottles floating in water, the ice long melted. I stuff the baseballs deeper into my pockets, kneel down beside the tub, and stick my hand into it. I fish around, pull out soda bottles one by one, and set them on the floor around the tub. Just as I've gotten the last one, I stop and cock my head to one side. Someone's behind me. Sweat pops out on my forehead and my heart starts beating faster.

"What you want, boy?"

It's a man's voice, deep and loud. I jump up, whirl around, and come face to face with a tall, slender white man in blue overalls and a red plaid shirt.

Mr. Luke Blackburn, I reckon.

I'm scared, but I look at him directly... straight in the eye, the way Papa Vee would. He's taller than I thought he'd be, and his white skin has brown spots all over it. His hair is reddish brown, the color of just-pulled sweet potatoes, unruly under a blue-and-white-striped baseball cap. A red mustache spreads over his top lip. He's a lot younger than I thought he would be—the same as Rev, or 'bout the age that Daddy Mo would be if he had lived.

"I *said*, what you want?" His voice is even louder this time.

I swallow hard. "Sodas."

Mr. Luke looks me up and down—likely noticing the baseballs stuffed in my pockets—and then his eyes suddenly widen, his face paling like he's seen a ghost. His eyes fix on Daddy Mo's baseball cap, then on the bottles I'm holding in my hands.

"That's a lot of sodas," he says at last. "Shouldn't you boys—all of you—be in school?"

I don't say anything, just gather up three sodas in the fingers of one hand, three in the fingers of the other, and head toward the front of the store. Mr. Luke's footsteps follow behind me. The back of my neck tingles, like spiders are crawling on it. When I get to the front, I stand at the counter next to Mason. Mr. Luke walks behind it, shoves his hands in the pockets of his blue overalls, and stares at the cap full of coins and the pile of peppermints.

Then he raises his head. "You're the spittin' image of your daddy, you know."

Me and Mason look at one another. I feel that knot in the pit of my stomach again. Did he know Daddy Mo? Is that why he's looking at me all funny? So I don't have to look back, I focus on the jars on the shelves behind him and pretend I didn't hear.

"Um, we want some nabs, please. Five cheese and six peanut butter," says Mason, his voice so low I can hardly hear him though I'm standing right next to him. I can see beads of sweat forming over his top lip.

Mr. Luke Blackburn is still staring at Daddy Mo's cap. "And what do you want, Li'l Moses?"

A rush of heat goes all through me. I take in a deep breath. Lordy! This white man knew Daddy Mo for sure!

I don't know what to make of this. Looking at him through narrowed eyes, I say, "My name is Cato." My heart beats fast. "We're buying these nabs here, eleven sodas, and the peppermints." I fix my gaze on the stack of candies on the counter 'stead of looking at Mr. Luke Blackburn.

"Don't stick your hand in the jar next time. I'll give you what you want. I fuss at my boy, Trace, for the same thing." Now he sounds like our teacher, Miss Holmes, when she's scolding us for something.

I don't say a word, but I steal a quick look at him. Red hair, spots on his skin, evil eyes. He looks like the Devil for sure.

Mr. Luke Blackburn gets two boxes of nabs from under the counter. "Six peanut butter and five cheese, you say?"

"Yes suh," says Mason.

Mr. Luke lays the nabs beside the cap full of coins, then looks at me again, tilting his head toward the back of the store.

"Are you going to get the rest of those sodas, boy?" His voice seems so unfriendly. My heart starts beating fast again.

"Yes suh," I say, walking to the back of the store. I carry the last five drinks to the front and put them on the counter.

"Um, suh, I want a sour pickle, too," says Mason.

I jerk my head around and glare at him.

"Hmm," says Mr. Luke Blackburn, pulling on one side of his sweet potato–colored mustache. "I'm low on pickles, boys. Want something else instead?" He looks back and forth between me and Mason.

"He only wants one," I say.

Mason cuts his eyes at me, sweat now rolling down his forehead. "That's all right. I don't want a pickle anymore."

"You don't want a pickle now? Well, I do," I say. "We'll have two sour pickles, please."

"You boys got money to pay for all of this?" Mr. Luke Blackburn looks straight at me.

"Oh, yes suh," Mason answers for me as he dumps the coins out.

Mr. Luke grabs one of the glass jars of pickles off the shelf behind him and places it on the counter. Sure enough, there's only a few in there. He opens it and picks up a fork.

"I want the big one in front, please suh." Mason points.

Mr. Luke's eyebrows shoot up. I know he heard, but he stabs a small pickle instead and holds it out.

"Um, he wants the big one," I say.

"This one's a nice mouthful and it only costs two cents," he says, waving the fork with its tiny pickle in the air.

Mason swallows so hard I can hear the sound in his throat.

When we don't say anything, Mr. Luke takes two pieces of brown paper and lays them on the counter. He holds the fork in front of Mason, and Mason plucks the tiny pickle off of it and wraps it in a sheet. Mr. Luke sticks the fork in the jar again and pulls out another pickle—this one even smaller than the last. Mason plucks that one off too and quickly wraps it up.

"We've got all we want," says Mason. "What do we owe?"

Mr. Luke Blackburn steps back from the counter and folds his arms across his chest.

"You tell me." He looks right at me. "Count it out yourself."

My blood rushes hot all through me. Feels like I'm on fire. This white man is testing us to see if we can figure.

I step up to the counter, divide the things we bought into separate piles, and place a pile of coins next to each one.

"Where's the money for the pickles?"

I keep my head down. Can't look at Mr. Luke. I want to choke the snot out of this man.

"Oh!" Mason pulls the baseball out of his front pocket, digs deep, and pulls out four cents. He lays the pennies on the counter. Mr. Luke gets a box from the shelf behind him and scrapes all the coins into it with his hand.

"Let's go," I say, grabbing as many sodas as I can carry off the counter. I head for the door.

"Boys? I know your friends are waiting outside. Go on to school now—I don't approve of cutting, and I don't allow loitering on my property."

I keep walking like I don't hear him.

"And don't slam the screen door when you go out. The hinges might come off."

Lordy. I hate the way Mr. Luke talks to us. We don't need scolding about slamming doors and such, especially from a white man we just paid good money to. I take in a deep breath, push on the screen with my shoulder, and go outside, Mason right behind me. We cross the road and go back to where the Rangers are waiting.

After me and Mason pass out the nabs and sodas, Mason says, "I need somebody to go back in with me, 'cause we couldn't carry all the sodas."

"I'll go," says Skeeter's cousin, Raymond D.

"Nah, you and Cato are too much alike," says Mason. "I need somebody with a cool head. Come on, Hank."

When they're back, Mason passes out the drinks, then gives me his own pack of peanut butter nabs. He thinks I'm mad 'cause he picked Hank to go with him, but I'm not mad at all.

"Let's eat, fellas," says Mason, ignoring what Mr. Luke said about loitering.

I glance at Mason and smile. Breaking a rule is a brave thing for him to do.

"Man! I'm thirsty. Where's the bottle opener?" asks Skeeter.

"Most stores have one on the outside corner," says Mason. "You know that."

Skeeter marches back across the road and looks around on the outside of the store until he finds a bottle opener. He pops the top off of his soda and guzzles it quickly. The rest of us rush over, open our soda bottles, then hurry back to our spot. I hope that Mr. Luke doesn't see us.

Skeeter watches us longingly as we drink our sodas and munch on our nabs. "Hmm. That soda was good! I could use another one."

"*No!* Ain't nobody going back in there!" Mason yells, surprising all of us.

"What about the deposit on our drink bottles?" asks Skeeter, bewildered. "A penny for each one—that's eleven cents."

"We need to go," insists Mason. "Hide the bottles in the field behind us and we'll pick them up on our way back."

"All right," says Skeeter. "Just don't want old man Blackburn to take them and get our money, that's all." He and his cousin, Raymond D., gather soda bottles from everyone and stash them under some bushes.

When they're done, I say, "Let's go, Rangers!"

The whole team and I start running toward Poplar Field—but then I stop and let them pass me. "I'll catch up!" I yell.

"What're you up to?" asks Skeeter, stopping just ahead of me.

"Nature calls, you know."

"Oh. Hey, CP handed your glove to me. Here it is," he says, passing it to me and then turning to catch up with the others.

I watch the Rangers 'til they're out of sight. Then I take the tiny sour pickle out of my back pocket, unwrap it, throw it on the ground, and mash it into the dirt with my shoe.

Ducking behind the bush, I fetch the bottles from where Skeeter and Raymond D. hid them. In my mind, I see Mr. Luke Blackburn steal the bottles, put the money from the deposit in the box with the rest of the coins we gave him, throw his head back, and laugh.

Now I'm mad all over again about the way he treated us.

I gather the bottles in a pile and look around for a rock just the right size. I find one sticking out of the ground, kind of flat on top. I raise it high and throw it down as hard as I can on the pile of soda bottles.

The sound of glass breaking is very satisfying.

I pick up the rock and smash it down on the bottles again and again, being careful not to cut my hands. Finally, all that's left is shards of glass scattered on the ground. When I'm done, I hurl the rock as far as I can. Just because.

Then I walk across the road and up the creaky steps to Blackburn's store. I open the screen door and slam it shut as hard as I can. The sound echoes in the stillness. Sure enough, one of the hinges breaks.

"Done," I whisper.

I take off running to catch up with the Rangers. But I can't help looking back at the store.

Oh lordy. Mr. Luke Blackburn is standing on the porch, watching me, his arms folded over his chest, his head cocked to one side. A wave of fear runs through me.

# Chapter 3
## NO TRESPASS

The Rangers have a good head start, so I'm running flat out to catch up with them. That could be why my heart is beating so fast—or it might be because I know that Mr. Luke Blackburn saw me leave the porch. He knows that I slammed the screen door. I wonder if he was watching when I broke the soda bottles, too.

Hey! They were ours, so it wasn't against the law.

Lordy. I've got to try and remember how to get to Poplar Field now. I'm looking for a clump of poplars with bark white enough to catch the eye: the narrow dirt path leading to the field is just past them.

*Here…Here it is!*

There's a big sign nailed to one of the trees: No TRESPASS, it says. I turn off onto the path anyway and make my way through the woods.

After a while, I come out into a clearing. I shade my eyes with both hands in the blinding sunlight, and see the Rangers standing together near home plate, staring at the ball field like they see the second coming.

"Criss-a-mighty! This ball field seems twice as big as ours," says Mason, holding his baseball cap over his chest.

"And there's plenty of good dirt to slide on, 'stead of crabgrass like we've got," adds CP.

I take in a deep breath and smell the dampness of Carolina clay. Poplar Field looks like the baseball diamonds on the postcards that my brother Isaac sends me from places like Chicago, Kansas City, and Pittsburgh. The ground is flat and smooth, like somebody swept it with a broom, and there's patches of grass in all the right places, 'stead of where you don't want them.

Then my eyes land on the pitcher's mound. It rises off the ground, its clean rubber plate waiting to be stomped hard before the first pitch is thrown.

CP breaks away from the rest of us, running around the bases. After he passes home plate for the fourth time, Mason calls, "What are you doing, man?"

"I'm Cool Papa Bell, seeing how fast I can run out here!"

"Heaven help you," says Mason, laughing. "You're gonna be drunk as a skunk from going in circles!"

"Look at the nice bleachers!" yells Skeeter. He races to the first row, sits down, bounces up again, moves to the second riser, and repeats. Soon the whole team is scrambling over the bleachers like squirrels climbing trees.

I run to the pitcher's mound, a wave of happiness rolling over me as I reach it and step on. I face home plate, then turn very slowly to look at all the bases, like I'm following a batter who just hit a home run.

I close my eyes and pretend that I'm at Comiskey Park in Chicago. Isaac told me all about it. I imagine I'm pitching in the 1939 East-West All-Star Game—the one he'll be playing in August, just a few months away.

*"Go Monarchs!"* I yell, surprising my own self.

The rest of the team runs onto the ball field, whooping and yelling. Everyone is excited—except Mason, who's started looking grim. He's standing near home plate, forehead wrinkled.

"What's the matter?" I ask.

"We're making too much noise, man. Somebody's gonna hear us."

"What? Let's just play ball, Mason."

"You know we're trespassing."

I roll my eyes. "We came out here to have fun."

Mason puts on his mitt and takes his place, squatting down in the catcher's spot. After I throw a few hard warm-up pitches to him, he finally smiles.

I smile back and feel the glow of friendship between us. Here, with my teammates, I'm safe. Nothing's going to happen today. I'm sure of it.

It's time to practice my newest windup. It looks a little crazy, but that's my style. First, I raise my left leg really high, so high it nearly grazes my cheek. Then, tilting, I release the ball. With all that power from my legs, it shoots out of my hand like a bullet, faster than I've ever thrown it. I stare at home plate, not quite believing how good a windup this is.

"Great pitch, man!" Mason hollers. Then, though he's not wearing a watch, he points to his wrist to let me know that time is passing. If we're going to have a match, it has to start. We all have to be home when school's supposed to let out.

We break into two small teams and play against each other for the next hour or so. After each side has two rounds of batting, we take a rest. Most of us lay in the grass, but Skeeter and Raymond D. climb all over the bleachers again.

Beside me, Mason glances at the far side of the field. There's a road there that goes deeper into New Hanover County.

"What *is* it, Mason?"

"We need to go. I've just got a feeling that we've been here too long."

"Lordy. I can count on you to ruin a good time." I stare at him hard. When he doesn't give, I sigh and say, "Oh, all right."

I put my fingers to my lips and whistle. Rangers rise out of the grass and come to home plate. "Time to go, fellas," I announce.

"*Nooooo!*" everybody yells at the same time.

"We just got here!" cries Skeeter.

"Yeah! We just got here!" echoes Raymond D.

"And now we'd better leave before our good time turns bad," I say firmly.

"Awwww," the Rangers groan.

I lead them toward the path we came in on. Rangers fall in behind me, but just as I get to the edge of the ball field, I step aside and let the rest of the team pass.

Skeeter stops. "What is it now? You coming?"

"In a minute."

They disappear into the woods. Poplar Field is still and peaceful with the others gone. Now I can hear the crickets in the grass and the birds in the trees. A Cooper's hawk circles overhead.

We played hard out here, and the bases are covered with dirt, so I pull a branch off of a sturdy tree and go brush them clean. There's plenty of footprints and slide marks on the infield, though, and I can't sweep *those* away. I wonder if somebody's gonna figure out we were here.

*Don't borrow trouble*, I tell myself.

I step onto the pitcher's mound one more time. There's still something special I have to do.

I take off Daddy Mo's cap and place it over my heart. I think about the locket Hope wears around her neck and the picture of Daddy Mo inside, the only one we have. He and my mama took it on the day they got married, Gran told me. I can feel him in my heart and see him in my mind: full lips, slender mustache, high cheekbones. We played catch at Walker Field. Sat at the kitchen table racing to see which one of us could eat the most molasses biscuits.

When I turn toward home plate, I pretend that Daddy Mo is standing beside me.

"Happy birthday," I whisper. "Here it is, the baseball field I wanted you to see." I raise both arms over my head and turn around in a circle so we can see all parts of the field.

"Wish the Rangers had a ball field like this. Wish we had a pitcher's mound raised off the ground like this one. Wish we had bleachers." I drop my head and let my arms fall to my side. "Lordy. I wish you were here."

My chest feels very full and my throat very tight. All of a sudden, tears roll down my cheeks and drip off my chin. I take in a deep breath, wipe my face with my shirtsleeve, put Daddy Mo's cap back on, and head home.

# Chapter 4
## MOLASSES BISCUITS

I'm proud of myself. I kept my promise to show Daddy Mo the white boys' new baseball field in New Hanover County. But that night, laying in bed, I'm uneasy—especially since Mason told me on the long walk home that he had a feeling somebody was watching us.

Worrying is making me queasy. Or maybe I'm just nervous that our teacher, Miss Holmes, will punish the Rangers for skipping school.

No matter. Don't regret a thing. I had to do what I did today, and the Rangers had to go with me. Couldn't do it by myself. Seems like I'd get used to Daddy Mo being dead, but I haven't.

That's 'cause something's missing. Don't know *how* he died, so I can't throw the last pebble of dirt on his grave. No one will tell me anything about it.

All this uneasiness keeps me tossing and turnin', but somehow I fall asleep anyway.

The next morning, I'm the first out of bed—on purpose, 'cause I don't want to talk to anybody. Gran and Papa Vee might ask me about school yesterday (and if Hope is someplace nearby, she'll make a face when she hears me lie). So I'm moving around the kitchen as quiet as can be, putting cold molasses biscuits into a paper sack for me and Mason. Then I sneak out the back door and around to the front yard.

*Dang!*

Papa Vee is sitting on the porch steps, whittling a piece of pinewood.

He sees me, so I sit down beside him. Don't have a choice, really. Holding the wood in his left hand and the knife in his right, he makes small cuts and lets the chips fall on the ground.

"What's in there?" He motions with his head, though I'm sure he already knows.

"Um…I brought you some molasses biscuits." I open the paper sack and tilt it toward him.

Papa Vee sets the wood and knife on the step beside him. He takes a biscuit and eats it in two bites. "Hmm! Nina's biscuits always taste good," he says. "And everything she cooks around Mo's birthday tastes extra special."

I tilt the bag again and Papa Vee gets another biscuit, licking molasses off his fingers when he's done. Then he picks up his knife and starts whittling again. "You can unpack your things, son."

"What…? What do you mean, Papa Vee?"

"I found your blanket roll and I looked inside. Your best pants, best shirts, clean socks, and underwear were all rolled up, neat as you please, like you're fixin' to go somewhere."

Oh. That.

"Wasn't trying to sneak around, Papa Vee." I take in a deep breath and blow it out slowly. "Isaac said he'd ask you when he got home."

"'Bout what?"

"If I can go to Kansas City with him…spend some time with the Monarchs, meet Mr. Satchel Paige." I'm holding my breath now.

"Uh-huh."

I look at Papa Vee sideways, then stare at the crickets jumping in the tall grasses of the yard. "Papa Vee? The bottom shelf of the pantry is mine. Why'd you look in my stuff?"

Never been this bold before. But going with Isaac is the most important thing to me right now.

Papa Vee wipes crumbs off his mouth with his shirtsleeve. "Boy, you ain't got no stuff. This is my house and everything in it belongs to me." His knife moves faster now, and pieces of wood fly every which way.

22

I can feel sweat popping out under my armpits. My heart beats faster. I want to yell at him, but I don't dare. Instead, my voice cracks when I say, "I'm almost thirteen. Old enough to have things of my own."

"Don't care how old you are or what you think is yours or not yours. You ain't going to Kansas City."

"Why? Isaac *wants* me to go with him. He said I can help out."

"Help with what?"

"Be in charge of the Monarchs bats, balls, and gloves—pass them out before every game and pick them up after," I say, making things up as I go. "Besides, going to Kansas City is the only way I can meet Mr. Satchel Paige! The best pitcher in Negro League baseball!"

Papa Vee stops whittling and looks at me with narrowed eyes. "Satchel will be around for a while. You'll meet him in due time, if that's what you want when you're grown." His voice softens. "Look, son, life on the road ain't easy for a baseball player. Isaac's got his hands full taking care of his own self."

I bite down hard on the inside of my lip until I taste blood in my mouth. "That's not what he says."

"Well...Your brother can't know the kind of burden you would be, Cato."

I stand and turn so I can look in Papa Vee's face. My hands ball up in tight fists.

"Isaac won't have to take care of me. I can take care of myself!" I'm shaking. I've *never* talked to Papa Vee like this. But I've never wanted anything so much, either. "Besides, Daddy Mo and Isaac left home when they were near my age!"

"No, son. Isaac was eighteen 'fore he ever set foot outside of Sycamore Grove, and your daddy was seventeen. And I shouldn't have let either one of them leave so young." Papa Vee looks past me—past the railroad tracks that run in front of the house—and out toward the highway in the distance. A convoy of Army trucks is headed to the base at Fort Bragg.

"Why do you say that?"

"Bad things can happen out there on the road, going from town to town."

"Out there? Bad things can happen *out there*?" I'm breathing hard now, tiny drops of spit fly out of my mouth. "The worst thing ever happened to Daddy Mo wasn't on the road. It was right here in Sycamore Grove!"

Papa Vee breathes in deep and loud. "I know that, son. And Sheriff Pridgeon never put a soul in jail for it."

"'Cause it was white men that killed him!"

Papa Vee's eyes are sad, and his hands begin to tremble. He moves the knife very slowly now.

"How did it happen? You and Gran and Rev whisper about things so me and Hope can't hear. You've *never* talked to us about how Daddy Mo died."

"I know. Colored folks have so many burdens in this world. I want you and Hope to play in the sunshine just a little longer."

"But I'm almost grown, Papa Vee! I deserve to know what happened. See, when I think of Daddy Mo, there's a stirrin' inside me. It's always there and I need to make it hush."

Papa Vee looks at me sideways. By now his piece of whittling wood is just a stick with no shape to it. Finally, he lays his knife down and throws the stick into the yard. "That stirrin' might never go away, son. Let it rest now. We've talked enough for one day."

I stare at him. There's a lot more to say!

But Papa Vee won't keep going, so I have to stop, too. A breeze rustles the grasses in the front yard. I close my eyes and draw the air deep into my lungs. When I open them, Gran is standing in the open front door. The look on her face tells me she heard everything—and that she knows how much I'm hurting.

"Another pan of biscuits just come out the oven," she says. "Taste mighty fine with some sweet molasses. Come on in the house and get some, Vee."

24

"After 'while," says Papa Vee.

I'm not shaking anymore, but I'm still mad. At myself this time, for the way I talked to Papa Vee. For disrespecting the man who raised me, the person I love more than anyone—except Gran and Hope and Isaac and Rev.

Standing over him like this, I can see that his hair is nearly white, his shiny bald spot much bigger than I remember. Tears fill my eyes, but I brush them away. I want to say how sorry I am, want to say that I see that he's hurting too. Instead, I sit back on the step beside him and look at the ground.

When Gran comes out carrying a plate of hot biscuits with molasses dripping down the sides, I let Papa Vee pick first, and I take the two that are left.

Our eyes meet for just a moment. We manage to smile.

Then we both stare toward the highway and eat our biscuits. Just as I lick the last sticky bit off my fingers, I see Mason running toward the house, waving his arms up and down.

# Chapter 5
## BOLD-FACED LIE

"What in the world is wrong with that boy?" asks Papa Vee.

"I'll find out."

I run toward Mason and he runs toward me, yelling, "Cato! He's coming, man!"

"*Who's* coming?"

"Mr. Luke Blackburn!"

I think about what I did at his store yesterday. "Why's he coming *here*!?"

"I betcha somebody saw us on that ball field," pants Mason, his eyes enormous. "Criss-a-mighty! What are we gonna do?"

Behind him, Mr. Luke Blackburn's gray pickup truck bobs up and down on the uneven dirt road like a boat on water. Me and Mason rush back to the house ahead of it.

"Mornin', Mister Vernon," says Mason, still sweating. "You think Miss Nina's got a molasses biscuit somewhere? I ran a long way…"

"There might be one left. You go on inside, son."

I sit down next to Papa Vee on the front porch steps as the pickup truck gets closer.

"Anything you want to tell me, son?"

"Uh…no suh." I swallow hard.

Like a child, I close my eyes and wish the truck would go away. Instead, it rolls into the yard and stops.

A boy about my age is driving. Certain without a license, 'cause he's too young, but nobody cares about breaking the law on these back roads. His shaggy sweet-potato-colored hair sticks out from under a blue-and-white-striped baseball cap.

Mr. Luke Blackburn gets out of the passenger side and walks up to the porch. My stomach feels like frogs are jumping around inside.

Papa Vee stands, facing Mr. Luke.

"Mornin', Vernon."

"Mornin', Luke. It's been a while."

"I know." Mr. Luke fumbles in the pocket of his overalls, pulls out a pipe, and taps it against his hand, then takes a small tin out of another pocket and stuffs tobacco into the pipe barrel. "How's Miss Nina?" he asks, smiling. "Just saying her name makes my mouth water for one of her peach pies."

"Yep. She does make good pies." Papa Vee nods.

Mr. Luke stops for a moment and looks around: at the house, at the yard, at the fields. "Your place looks good, Vernon. Nate and Ollie still helping out?"

"Yep," says Papa Vee.

Mr. Luke pulls out a book of matches and lights the pipe. His cheeks sink in as he draws on it. White smoke comes out of his mouth and rises into the air.

For a moment, Papa Vee's eyes soften, and a smile plays around the corners of his mouth. "Using Prince Albert tobachy just like your daddy, I see."

"Like you used to, Vernon." Mr. Luke looks directly at Papa Vee for the first time. He clears his throat. "Your boy came by my store yesterday. He was with a bunch of fellas. It was morning, so I figured they were either *very* late to school, or…well…they were all skipping."

"I see." Papa Vee glances my way before he looks at Mr. Luke again. "But I know you didn't come here after all this time to tell me Cato skipped school."

After he takes a long drag on his pipe, Mr. Luke blows the smoke to the side, away from Papa Vee's face. "I found out that when your boys left my store they went over to my new baseball field. It's a beauty, Vernon. Call it Poplar Field. You ought to see it." Mr. Luke's eyes look far away for a moment. "And, well, I put up a 'No Trespass' sign, big as day, but your boy and his pals paid no mind to it, sliding in the dirt and carrying on. But the worst part is there was a lot of damage when they left: broken glass, bases pulled out of the ground and thrown to the side. My boy and his teammates had to clean up before they could even have baseball practice."

*What?* Liar! I broke the soda bottles near his store, not on the ball field! And Rangers would *never* mess up a ball field. Chills run down my back at just the thought of doing something so vile. I even swept when we finished!

Papa Vee glances at me again. "Cato, were you boys on Luke's property?"

My mouth goes bone-dry. "We…we just wanted to take a look, Papa Vee. We didn't do any harm to it, I swear."

"Don't swear, son," says Papa Vee.

Mr. Luke takes another long drag on his pipe and lets the smoke curl up in the air. "My boy, Trace, says different. He says the ball field was fine the day before, but it was all tore up yesterday afternoon."

Papa Vee motions to the house. "Cato, go tell Mason to come out here."

"Yes suh."

As I walk, the boy in the pickup truck points his finger at me and snickers.

*You bold-faced liar. I wish I could get my hands on you!*

I poke my head in the front door. Mason is listening just inside, like I knew he would be, and I motion for him to follow me. There's no pleasantries this time: Papa Vee looks right at Mason. "Luke says the Rangers were on his ball field yesterday, Mason. Is that so?"

Mason looks at me, then back at Papa Vee. His eyes are 'bout to pop out of his head. He kicks at the ground, stalling, but finally says, "Yes suh, Mr. Vernon. But we just ran around and threw some balls. That's all."

Mr. Luke Blackburn sucks in his breath, loudly. "This ain't no back and forth."

"I know that, Luke," says Papa Vee, a sharpness in his voice.

Mr. Luke's eyebrows shoot up for a moment, then drop. He bites down hard on the pipe stem.

"So what do you want to do, Luke?" asks Papa Vee.

"Because he's your boy, Vernon, we can take care of this ourselves. But I can't just let it go. These boys need to learn what a 'No Trespass' sign means. If they ignore another one, awful things could happen."

"Tell me what you want them to do."

"Well, no need to be heavy-handed, Vernon. We can just teach them a lesson."

Papa Vee leans his head to the side. "What you got in mind, Luke?"

"Work. I've got some unloading to do at my store. It would take Trace two days to finish, but your boys could do it in a morning, easy." Mr. Luke's pipe has gone out now. He takes a match and lights it again. "They'll learn the lesson they already know all over again. If you do wrong, there's a price to pay."

Papa Vee nods.

Mr. Luke pulls in a deep breath of smoke and lets it out slowly. "You know, Vernon, when I saw your boy the other day, and found out he loved baseball, well...it brought Moses to my mind."

Papa Vee's body stiffens. But he keeps his face still, and after a while, his shoulders relax again. "You want the whole team to do those chores you mentioned?"

"No. Just these two. They're the ones who came inside to buy sodas."

"When do you want them?"

"Tomorrow morning."

"They'll be there." Without another word, Papa Vee turns and heads inside.

Mr. Luke watches him for a moment, then walks back to his truck and gets in. The sweet-potato-headed boy stares at me and Mason, grinning. Then he turns the truck around in the yard and drives off.

Man! I would love to see the Rangers whip the tar out of that white boy and his team right on their own fancy ball field. Just one fair game, and we could do it. Easy.

Me and Mason watch the gray pickup truck disappear. He's silent and so am I.

Lordy! What a mess we're in! And Papa Vee didn't get us out of it either.

Hope warned me about this. Can't my sister be wrong *sometimes*?

# Chapter 6
## CAT'S PAW

Next morning, the early air feels damp and cool as I leave the house. Man! Baseball season will be starting soon, and it would be a great day for the Rangers to practice, but me and Mason have work to do at Mr. Luke Blackburn's store.

"Cato! You plan on moving today, man?" Mason calls to me from the road.

I walk down the porch steps and we head to Blackburn's store, keeping a steady pace, looking straight ahead, not talking like we normally do. When we've walked a few miles, we spot the store in the distance. Mason stops, and I do too.

"Criss-a-mighty!" he whispers, shaking his head.

Four white boys sit on the steps, talking to one another and laughing. When they see us, they stand up all at once.

There's Mr. Luke's son, Sweet Potato Head, out front, but the fella walking next to him—wearing a blue-and-white-striped baseball cap, just like his—seems in charge. He's taller than all of us, and he looks older too. His wide shoulders stretch the buttons on his red plaid shirt, and his arms are thick as lumber, ready to break something—or someone—into kindling.

The skin on the back of my neck tingles.

"I ain't too proud to run," says Mason, huddling closer to me.

"Won't be no running," I say. "There's only four of them."

"Looks more like three boys and a locomotive."

The boys stroll over, stopping right in front of us. Up close, Sweet Potato Head looks so much like Mr. Blackburn it surprises me. His eyes are a darker green, but that wild hair poking out from under his cap, the color of sweet potato skin and Carolina clay, marks him as a Blackburn for sure.

"You boys don't look up to a hard day's work," says Sweet Potato Head, crossing his arms in front of him.

The locomotive curls his upper lip. "You's some of the weakest looking neegas I ever seen."

Oh my lordy. Hearing that word makes me madder'n a hound dog full of buckshot.

Me and Mason look at one another, and I can tell he's not too happy either.

Still, though, we don't say a word.

Not even when the tall one laughs, showing a wide gap where one of his front teeth used to be. "This is what you get for trespassing and being...uh, what did Mr. Luke say, Trace?"

"Vandals, Freight Train. Daddy called them vandals. Fellas that destroy other people's property." Trace Blackburn turns his head to the side and wrinkles up his nose, like he smells something bad. "You're ball players and you do this?"

"So, you's trespassers and vandals too." Freight Train folds his arms across his chest, just like Trace.

"*Liar!*" The word flies out of my mouth before I know it. I curl my hands into fists, then take a deep breath and hold it so my chest looks bigger.

"Nuh uh!" yells Sweet Potato Head. He leans forward, arm raised, finger pointing to the sky. "Freight Train and his cousins *saw* what you did to our ball field."

Mason puts a steadying hand on my shoulder. I remember what he said about somebody watching us.

"Me and my cousinsr—Digger and Mouse, here—spent half a day cleaning up the trash you boys left." Freight Train gestures at the two boys behind him, both wearing red T-shirts. They start to laugh, but it's more like dogs howling. "You's ours for the day, and we're gonna make you pay for what you did!"

"Li-*ar*," I say—louder this time, making it sound like two words.

Freight Train fixes a stare on me. His cousins stop laughing. "Who you callin' a liar, neega?"

That word again!

Digger and Mouse step up next to Freight Train, arms stiff at their sides. Mason's hand is still on my shoulder, and he squeezes me.

Trace Blackburn steps in front of the other white boys. "Daddy left me in charge." He motions for his crew to wait under a tree out back, then waves to me and Mason. "You boys, come with me."

Me and Mason follow Trace toward the store, Freight Train and his cousins walking behind us by just a few steps. They peel off to sit on empty crates under the tree, and Trace points me and Mason to an old pickup truck with chipped black paint. Boxes are piled on the cargo bed.

"Daddy wants you to unload this truck, haul the boxes inside, and set them on the floor in the back. When you're done with all that, I'll show you where to put everything on the shelves."

*Yes, Li'l Massa.*

Trace stares at me and Mason. We stare back.

"What they call you boys?" he asks after a moment.

"Cato Jones, pitcher for the Pender County Rangers," I say, touching my chest with my thumb. "We're the best baseball team in eastern Carolina. And this here is Mason, our catcher."

Trace looks down, grins, and shakes his head. "You may be the best colored team in colored town, but you see this blue and white?" He takes off his blue-and-white-striped baseball cap and shoves it at us. "The New Hanover Marlins are the best baseball team in *all* of Carolina, period. I'm the pitcher—and the captain."

Lordy. White boys think they're the best at everything.

"Well, Cato's so good, he was invited up north to play with the Newark Eagles this summer," says Mason.

I look at him. That's a pretty good lie.

"That's just a colored team, right?" Trace sniffs. "But you boys can't really love the game—not like we do. Not after seeing what you did to our *brand-new* ball field!" He nearly spits out these last words, then turns and walks away.

I get hot again, but Mason sees and grabs both my arms. "Let it go, man. We don't need any more trouble than we already got."

Part of me agrees, and so me and Mason start hauling boxes into the store. Trace and the other boys sit under the tree, pitching rocks and talking. The stench of cigarette smoke drifts through the air. Freight Train is the only one watching us.

"Them boys give me the willies—especially the big one," whispers Mason.

"Amen to that," I whisper back.

We work silently, and we seldom look at the boys under the tree. After a while, Trace Blackburn gets up and walks toward the woods. "I'll be right back."

Soon as he's gone, Freight Train lifts up the box he's sitting on and takes something out from under it. Him and Digger and Mouse stand in a circle, cigarettes dangling from their mouths. They start playing some kind of game, tossing something from one to the other.

I hear a whimper, then see a golden ball of fur rise in the air.

"Oops!" says Freight Train as a kitten falls to the ground on its side. When it tries to scramble to its feet, Freight Train grabs it by the scruff of its neck and throws it to one of his cousins.

Oh my lordy! I think that's Hope's kitten, Moses, the one she named for Daddy Mo!

"*Hey!*" I yell. I know I'm prob'ly starting trouble, but I can't help it. "*Leave it alone!*"

Freight Train stops, looks at me, then holds the kitten high in the air.

"I bet I can make this critter dance," he drawls, pulling hard on his cigarette until the end burns red-hot. Then he holds the cigarette a ways from the kitten's belly, moving it closer and closer.

When the cigarette is an inch away, he pauses.

"Mercy! I can't do this." He winks at me, still grinning. "Wait. Yes I can."

I swallow hard, thinking of Hope. It feels like a wildfire is rushing up from my toes to the tip of my nose.

Mason comes outside for another box. It probably only takes him a second to figure out what's going down. "They're playing with you, Cato, trying to start something! He hasn't hurt that kitten and he ain't gonna!"

Freight Train looks first at me, then at Mason. Then he grinds the burning cigarette right into the kitten's belly.

The kitten's cries pierce the air. It tries to fold into a ball to protect itself. For a moment, I shut my eyes and drop my head, not wanting to see a critter suffer like this—

—but then I find myself running toward Freight Train.

He doesn't react as I snatch the kitten out of his hands, but I can tell his mind is catching up to what has just happened. I back away, real slow, figuring to take off running. Next thing I know, Mason is standing between us, arms spread out to protect me.

With one sweep of his thick arm, Freight Train shoves Mason to the ground. "You gone too far, neega boy! I'm-a break every bone in your body now!"

"*Freight Train!*" Trace Blackburn suddenly rushes between us. "Look-a-here, these boys need to unload this truck 'fore Daddy gets back. Leave them alone and let them work." His voice is loud and firm.

Freight Train leans to the side so he can look right at me. He glares for a moment. "You ain't no fun, Trace Blackburn." Slowly, he walks over to me, grabs the kitten out of my hands, and carries it back to his seat under the tree, stroking its back gently. The kitten is still wailing.

"Y'all need to hurry up," says Trace, looking from me to Mason to Freight Train and his cousins.

"You ain't got to worry 'bout that," mutters Mason, rushing to pick up another box off the truck.

Me and Mason go back and forth between the truck and the store three more times until all but one of the boxes is inside. When Trace sees that we're almost done, he yells from his seat under the tree, "Hey! I'd better show you where Daddy wants things on the shelves."

*Thank you, Li'l Massa.* We head inside and pretend to listen carefully.

"Daddy wants the big cans of lard on the bottom shelves, the sacks of flour and cornmeal on the middle shelves, and the smaller bags of beans on the top. You understand me?"

"Yes suh, Mr. Trace," I say, holding my head down and nodding vigorously.

"I'll check everything when you're done," says Trace, seeming puzzled at my willingness as he walks out the door.

"Cato, you need to stop making fun of white folks right to their face!" Mason sounds so serious, but then we both bust out laughing. Nervous laughing. From then on, me and Mason work like somebody's holding a shotgun on us. Neither one of us says a word until we're done.

"You make a pretty good slave, Mr. Brown," I say.

"So do you, Mr. Jones." We fall out laughing again.

"Wait. There's one more box on the truck. I'll get it," I say.

Mason lets out a long breath. "Hurry up, man."

Back outside, I grab the box off the truck bed. I try to ignore Trace and the others, but I can't help stealing a glance at them. They're all standing close to the tree, looking up at something. I follow their gaze.

At first I can't figure out what I'm looking at—but then I let go of the box and it drops with a thud. I cover my mouth with both hands.

*No!*

A yellow ball of fur is dangling from a branch high in the tree, hanging from a noose.

The kitten! Its paws are curled up close to its body, and its tiny head droops to one side. I think it's a goner, when all a sudden, its legs flail about wildly—almost like it's running to free itself from the rope around its neck. For the love of God...!

My stomach feels queasy. I spit on the ground. Would spit on *them* if I could!

Freight Train and his cousins laugh, but Trace is standing stiff, his forehead wrinkled, his fists balled, his arms close to his sides. He turns toward me, and our eyes meet for just a moment. The pain I'm feeling shows on his face too.

"Enough of this!" he yells.

Quickly, he stacks a couple of loose crates on top of one another, climbs up, lifts the kitten's body with one hand, and loosens the rope around its neck with the other. I rush to him and raise my arms up to take the little critter. When Trace puts the kitten in my hands, it's not moving, but I feel its heart beating against my palm.

Freight Train slaps his sides. "What is wrong with you, Trace Blackburn? It's just a kitten, man! What you gonna do when we invite you to a real party, huh?"

I ignore the lot of them and rush back into the store, holding the kitten gently in my hands. Lordy. Me and Mason need to leave this place. Now!

"Cato? Oh man! They really *did* hurt it. Why?"

I don't say a word, just grab him, rush out the front door, and take off running for home.

Sweat pours off of me, and my heart is beating so fast, seems it might jump out of my chest. Every colored boy growing up in the South knows that when a white man brings out a rope, nothing good comes after that.

Nothing!

# Chapter 7
## FAMILY TIES

Me and Mason walk a long time in silence before we speak.

"Criss-a-mighty, Cato! Those are some mean white boys!" I see him shudder.

"Mean is one word for it."

"At least Trace knew what was right."

After that, neither one of us says another word.

In my mind, I can still hear little Moses wailing from the pain of that cigarette burn, still see him fighting for his life as the rope around his neck got tighter. I glance down at him. He's sleeping, and I'm so relieved to feel his pulse beating against my palm. But that only makes me think more about what happened. I feel sick all over again.

I breathe in, letting clean, fresh air fill up my lungs, but it doesn't help. I *still* feel sick.

Soon, me and Mason come to a fork in the road.

"Take this little critter home with you, Mason. We can't let Hope see what they did to it." I pass Moses to Mason, and he cradles it gently. "I'll come over and feed him, take care of him. 'Til he's better for Hope."

"Nah, man. I'll nurse the kitty back to health. Hope's like my little sister too."

I gaze at Moses one last time, then nod, pat his shoulder, and turn down the path to my house. Mason keeps walking to his.

Papa Vee is sitting on the porch steps, whittling, when I get home. I sit down beside him and stare at his hands.

"Did Luke try to work you boys to death this morning?" he asks.

"Mr. Luke wasn't there. Just his son, Trace, and three other white boys." My heart is pounding. *Should I tell?*

"So, what did Luke have you boys doing?"

"We unloaded boxes from his truck, carried them inside, and put the food on shelves."

Papa Vee laughs under his breath. "That's all? Luke was mighty easy on you and Mason."

For a while, me and Papa Vee sit quietly. His knife moves faster now. The wood he's carving looks more like a small bird with each stroke.

"You say there were four white boys at the store? Anything happen I ought to know about?"

I start to sweat again. "Like what?"

"Like whatever makes your leg jiggle up and down the way it's been doing ever since you sat down. Like whatever it is that makes you ask me a question 'stead of telling me what went on."

I bite down hard on my lower lip to keep the tears back. I want to lie, just so I don't have to talk about it, but I can't. It's too big to lie. "They tortured Hope's kitten, Papa Vee."

He's quiet a minute. "Didn't know she had one."

"It was just a stray that started coming 'round here a few days ago. Hope's been feeding it. And she named it Moses."

"So what happened to it...eh...to Moses?"

"Well...first they burned it with a cigarette." My voice shakes. "Then they put a rope around its neck and dangled it from a tree."

Papa Vee stops whittling. He takes in a breath so deep and loud that I look up at him. "Was Luke's boy there?"

"Yes suh."

"And where's the cat now?"

"Mason has it. He said he'll nurse it." I swallow. "We didn't want Hope to see what they did to her critter."

Papa Vee lays the knife and the piece of wood down on the porch step beside him. His hands are trembling. "We're going to pay a visit to Mr. Luke Blackburn this evening, son. Soon as your chores are done."

I don't say nothing, but something makes me wish my chores last a long, long time.

———

Daylight's fading when me and Papa Vee get to Mr. Luke's store. Two white men are there, buying a last few things before the store closes. Trace is in the yard, loading sacks onto the back of a red pickup truck. He watches me as we drive up, then disappears inside. When he comes out again, Mr. Luke is with him. They both wave at a man in the red truck, the last one to leave.

Mr. Luke walks out to meet us. "Evening, Vernon."

"Evening, Luke," says Papa Vee.

"Your boys did a fine job this morning," says Mr. Luke. "They left a few boxes in the middle of the floor, but that's all right."

Papa Vee looks over Mr. Luke's shoulder at Trace, standing on the porch. "I've got something I want to talk about, Luke."

"Sure Vernon. Trace, bring another chair out. We've got company."

Trace's eyebrows shoot up. He looks at Mr. Luke, then he looks at Papa Vee, then he opens the screen door and disappears inside. He comes back carrying a straight-back chair with a straw bottom.

"You take the rocker, Vernon," says Mr. Luke, leading us up the porch steps. He grabs the straight-back chair from Trace and straddles it, sitting backward. "Now get us some sodas, son."

"Give him a hand, Cato," says Papa Vee.

Trace stares at Mr. Luke, forehead creased, but he motions me inside.

Once I'm in the door, all the memories from this morning come back. My mouth goes dry—I can't believe I'm in this awful place again! I stumble over one of the boxes me and Mason left on the floor before we ran out.

Trace whirls around to face me, fire in his eyes. "What're you here for?"

"You oughta know."

Trace takes a step toward me. "You told?"

I glare at him. This white boy's got some nerve, getting up in my face.

"You don't have to tell grown folks *everything*. It was just a stray cat that nobody cared about."

"My sister cares about it."

Trace jerks back like somebody spit in his face. The anger falls right off of him. "That was your sister's cat?"

"Sure is. It would break her heart if she found out what you fellas did to it. She named it Moses."

Trace's cheeks turn red. "Is it...I mean...?"

"Alive. But barely."

"Well, then. What's done is done." He pulls in his lower lip and bites down on it. "We'd better get these sodas outside."

We pull four bottles from the washtub on the floor, pop the caps off with the bottle opener on the wall, and walk back out to the front porch. Mr. Luke is standing on the edge of it and turns to face us with a look that sends chills all through me.

I'm not sure I understand why, but his lower lip is trembling. Maybe even Trace doesn't know. He's right beside me and I can hear him suck in a deep breath.

Mr. Luke clears his throat and reaches for the Pepsi-Cola in Trace's hand. I give Papa Vee a Co-Cola.

Me and Trace sit down on opposite ends of the porch steps to drink our Nehi orange and grape sodas. Soon as he turns his up, I see that he means to race me—so I put my lips clear around the neck of the bottle, tilt my head way back, and guzzle. When I'm done, I lower the bottle and look at him.

Dang it! A tie! For a moment, it seems like both of us will smile. But we don't.

Mr. Luke sits in his chair. "I sure miss the old days, Vernon," he says. "They were good days too. Our families were always close. You and Miss

Nina were the only colored people Daddy let come through the front door of this store."

"If memory serves me, Luke, we never did use the priv'lege, though your daddy allowed it. Nina and me was waiting for the day when all colored folks could walk through the front door."

Mr. Luke's eyes drop to the floor. For a while he doesn't say anything. Then all a sudden, he yells out, "Trace!"

Me and Trace both jump.

"Yes sir?"

"What happened here at the store this morning?"

Trace's eyes dart around wildly. "What do you mean, Daddy?"

Mr. Luke's teeth clench. "Boy, I asked you a question."

"Well…" Sweat shines on Trace's face. He scratches his arm, leaving red marks. "Freight Train and his cousins were playing with this stray cat."

"Tell me the whole story, son."

"Well, they were playing with this cat…and then somehow…it got a noose around its neck. I don't think they meant to do it."

"*Have mercy!*" Mr. Luke yells, rising so fast his chair falls over on the porch. "Son, hanging is the kind of thing a body has to *think* on. Ain't no accident!"

"But Daddy! *I* didn't let them hang it!"

Mr. Luke stares at Trace, tight lines across his forehead and around his mouth. After a long time, he rights his chair and sits again. "How did this all start?"

"I went inside to make sure the fellas were stacking the shelves right. That's when it happened."

"But I left you in charge, Trace. Everything falls on you."

"Yes sir." Trace's voice is so low, we can barely hear him. His shoulders slump, and he looks down at the step he's sitting on.

"Who all was here, Trace?" asks Mr. Luke.

"Freight Train and his cousins, Digger and Mouse."

"Hmm. I'm going to have a talk with Freight Train, and his mouth had better know how to say 'I'm sorry.' If he does anything like this again, he's off the team."

"Yes sir."

Then Mr. Luke looks right at Trace. "I expect a whole lot more from you, son. You're a Blackburn, descended from fine Republican stock. We're the kind of people that risk our lives to make the South a better place—along with colored folks."

Mr. Luke pauses, turns to look at Papa Vee, and takes a long swallow of his Pepsi-Cola.

"Our families go way back, the Blackburns and the Joneses. After slavery was done, about the mid-nineties, I'd say, Vernon's granddaddy and your great-granddaddy were both elected aldermen for the city of Wilmington. White and colored were running the city together then."

Me and Trace look at one another. His eyes are wide, and I can tell he's as surprised as I am.

"That was too much for some people. It was all broken up in a hail of gunfire, sending good people scattering for other parts of Carolina—or out of the South altogether. We stayed, made do with how things were. But we still believe in justice, Trace. We're nothing like the kind of riffraff that tries to scare colored folk, the kind that uses ropes to do the Devil's work."

"Yes sir," says Trace, digging his fingernails into his arm, drawing blood.

"And I don't want to see Freight Train or his cousins 'round this store anymore, you hear me?"

"Yes sir."

Trace glances at me, his cheeks and forehead red as can be. I remember how he snickered when I was in trouble, but I won't laugh at him now.

Mr. Luke sets his soda bottle on the porch, takes out a white kerchief, and wipes his face and neck. "It's not the end of this, Trace. We've got a lot of talking to do."

The evening air is still, the only sounds crickets chirping in the bushes and Papa Vee's rocker creaking. There's just enough light for us to see one another now.

"One more thing, Vernon," says Mr. Luke. "Your boys got into trouble because they wanted to see Poplar Field. I wish somebody had asked."

"Hard to ask something of a ghost, Luke."

"I know, Vernon. And I'm sorry for staying away like I have. From now on, if you want something, just ask me."

My head jerks around. I stare hard at this man that I've been scared of for so many years. He would've let us on the field? All we had to do is ask?

It's nothing like I thought.

I take a deep breath. "Mr. Luke? Can the Rangers practice on your new ball field sometime?"

"Sure you can, son. Even better, your team can practice with the Marlins—that'll clear the air. They'll be there on Saturday next week. How about it?"

I turn and look at Trace. His eyes are bugging, and his face is even redder than before.

My eyes narrow, and my mouth curls up on one side. "What time?" I ask him.

Trace's gaze drops. He mumbles something.

"Say what?" I ask loudly.

"*Ten o'clock*," he shouts, his cheeks going cherry red.

"Well now, look at that! Why, if you boys play ball together, you're gonna love it, just like me and Mo did."

"Sounds good to me," says Papa Vee, getting up from the rocker.

Mr. Luke gets up right after him and puts his hand on Papa Vee's shoulder. "It was really great seeing you, Vernon. Seemed like the old days when Mo was still with us."

"Yep," says Papa Vee.

"Now, Mo and me weren't quite as close as you and Daddy…"

"I reckon not. I worked for Luther since I was twelve years old."

"But I want you to know that I will never have another friend like Moses." Tears form in Mr. Luke's eyes. "I miss him every day."

"We all do, Luke. Thanks for the soda." Papa Vee walks down the steps to his pickup truck, and I follow. He gets in on the rider's side, which means I should climb into the driver's seat and start the engine. I do, and we turn out of the yard and down the back road for home, leaving Trace and Mr. Luke standing on the porch.

Me and Papa Vee don't talk about what just happened, but my mind is spinning. Papa Vee worked for Mr. Luke's daddy, Luther—and they were *friends*? Mr. Luke and Daddy Mo were friends too? Mr. Luke *misses* Daddy Mo?

I glance at Papa Vee sideways, knots forming in my stomach. How come I don't know about any of this? How did Mr. Luke get such a bad reputation?

And what else is Papa Vee hiding from me?

# Chapter 8
## TWO PEAS FROM THE SAME POD

When we get home, I go straight into the house looking for something to eat. Gran is in the kitchen, but there's no food on the table; the pots are sitting on the stove behind her. We're late for supper, and whatever we eat we'll have to get ourselves.

I spot Gran's medicine bag in a chair nearby. In this house, we know what that means. Somebody's sick. Not deathly sick, or Gran wouldn't be here, but sick enough. Most likely, she and Papa Vee will drive away in the early hours of the morning to the person's house, where her healing partner, Miss Mary Agnes, will meet her.

Gran herself is sitting at the table, a small bowl in front of her with Mason jars in a semicircle around it. Each jar has some kind of powder inside and a spoon next to it. Once a month, Gran checks her ground-up plants and herbs to make sure she has enough to make the poultices, salves, and teas that she uses to heal people—to bring down fevers and swelling, or to treat a rash, like poison ivy. Gran can set broken bones; cure pneumonia, or the croup; and help folks that's got pain and swelling in their teeth. She also brings lots of babies into the world.

Every now and again, Gran drags me and Hope outside to forage. Hope loves this chore, 'cause she wants to be a healer just like Gran, but I don't take kindly to anything that keeps me off the baseball field for too long.

My stomach is making noises something awful now, so I walk over to the stove, lift the lid on the big cast-iron pot, and find chicken and vegetable stew so thick that a spoon would stand straight up in it. There's a pan of cornbread with cracklings on the stove too, with two corner squares missing.

"Don't be greedy now." Gran's voice is firm, but she doesn't even look up at me. "Your granddaddy's got to eat. And you need to save something for Amos in case he comes by."

"Yes'm."

I sit in the chair opposite Gran so that none of my food can get into her powders. (Or the other way 'round.) After three hardy spoonfuls of stew and a hunk of cornbread, my eyes fall on Gran's busy hands. I've seen her do this a hundred times, but never asked questions.

Finding out how much I didn't know about Mr. Luke and Daddy Mo, about Papa Vee and Mr. Luke's daddy—well, that taught me a lesson today.

"Um, Gran…"

"Shush! My mind's occa'pied."

"Yes'm." I finish the rest of my stew and cornbread.

After a while, Gran fills a pint jar with the blend of powders that she mixed in the bowl, screws a lid on it, and ties a yellow ribbon around it. Then she places both hands on the table, lets out a long breath, smiles, and turns her gaze on me.

"What you want, son?"

"How long have you been a healer, Gran?"

Her eyes light up when I ask. "All my life. From the age of six, I was mama's shadow. She was a healer and her mama before her. Our family was known for healing in New Orleans."

"Were all the women in your family healers?"

"No. My sister, Kate, was a seamstress. She brought in so much money that nobody bothered her 'bout healing."

"Did you learn to sew?"

"Ha! My grandma tried to teach me, but I was all thumbs. Now your sister, Hope, she's got a heart for healing and a hand for stitching. They've got doctors like that; call them surgeons."

Now I've started, the questions keep tumbling out of me. "Did you ever want to be a doctor, Gran?"

"I *am* a doctor. Me and Miss Mary Agnes both. When you got the power of life and death in your hands like we do, well, you're a doctor no matter what the gov'ment says."

Right then, Hope rushes into the kitchen carrying a small cardboard box. "Gran! Look what I found at the foot of the oak tree out back. Got it just in time too. A garden snake was slitherin' toward it."

Hope sets the box down on the table and sits in the chair across from me. Both Gran and me stretch our necks to see what's inside. It's the tiniest bird I've ever seen. Looks like it just hatched. Its eyes are closed and it's still as death.

Gran narrows her eyes, cocks her head to the side, and looks straight at Hope. "How you know the little critter's alive, honey?"

"I felt its heartbeat when I picked it up, Gran."

"Well now, I want you to get a paper bag and go back outside. Gather some more dirt and weeds to lay in the box with the little birdy. When he gets back to his mama's nest, he needs to smell like her 'stead of you."

Hope's eyes widen. "What?"

Gran lays her hand on Hope's shoulder and squeezes. "If this robin smells like Hope when you put it back in the nest, his mama will let it die, sweetie. It'll be a sign he don't belong in the family."

"Oh." Tears form in Hope's eyes.

"Cato, go outside with your sister and help her gather up some weeds and dirt to put in the box."

"Yes'm." I get up from the table, grab a paper bag out of the pantry, and head for the back door. "Come on, Hope. When we tell Miss Holmes about your adventure, can't say you were cryin' now."

Hope wipes her face with both hands, pops up out of the chair, grabs the paper bag from my hand, and heads toward the door. "I better write this down 'fore I go to bed so I can tell Miss Holmes the whole story."

Gran smiles and winks at me as I follow my little sister outside.

Hope rushes over to the oak tree and falls onto her knees. She begins scooping dirt up and shoving it into the paper bag.

"Hey! Ain't no rush. Let me help," I say. "Be a couple of days 'fore that bird can go home. Besides, ain't nothin' bad going to happen with Gran watching over it."

Hope drops the paper bag and sits with her rear resting on her ankles. When I look close, tears are rolling down her cheeks.

"Hope? What is wrong with you today? All of this cryin' ain't like you, girl."

She takes in a deep breath. "Never told anyone, but I'm easy to cry 'round the time of Daddy Mo's birthday."

I've been so busy thinking about how much *I* miss Daddy Mo, I forgot about my little sister.

I put my hand in the middle of her back and rub circles, just like Gran does for me.

Hope turns toward me, and I put my arms around her. Don't know what else to do. "Why did Daddy Mo have to die? Why'd Mama die birthin' me? Do you know?" She grips my shirt. "Sometimes it almost seems I—killed her."

My heart stops. For a moment, I can't breathe. "What are you talking about, Hope?"

"Gran made it sound like I was gonna kill that little robin too!"

She starts crying harder, crying until she's choking on her sobs.

"Okay, listen here, little sister. I'm gonna talk to you like Miss Holmes would." I hold her tight. "First off, you want to be a healer like Gran, so it's her job to tell you what you need to know. It wasn't to hurt you."

I cuddle her until she's all cried out. Hope's breathing comes slower now.

"Next, you're not the only one that cries 'round Daddy Mo's birthday. We all do. I've even heard Papa Vee shed a tear in the wee hours. And don't get me started 'bout Rev!"

That makes Hope laugh, a little.

"Last thing. Gran has delivered a lot of babies and sometimes the mamas go to heaven. *Never question the life that the good Lord has given us*, she says. Don't know why Daddy Mo was taken from us, too, but Gran and Papa Vee are 'bout the best folks in the whole wide world to be living with."

"Ain't that the truth," Hope whispers.

"Anytime you feel lonesome, just give one of 'em a big hug and see if you don't feel better."

For a while, we sit quietly just holding one another, until we hear, "*Cato! Hope!* Y'all comin' back anytime soon?"

"Uh-oh. Double time!" I say. Hope manages a smile.

We scramble to fill the paper bag with dirt and weeds, then hurry back inside.

# Chapter 9

## SHADOW BALL

It's been a week since me and Papa Vee paid a visit to Mr. Luke at his store. A week since I learned how close our families were, once upon a time. I was hoping that Papa Vee would sit me down and tell the whole story. He hasn't done that and I'm too scared to ask.

Mostly, it's all I can think about. Today, though, I can put it out of my mind. The Rangers get to play on Poplar Field—even if it means we have to practice with the Marlins.

"Cato, have you seen my kitty? Moses hasn't been coming around, and I'm worried. Robbie Robin's been needing a lot of care, but I can tend to Moses too."

Hope is sitting at the kitchen table eating apple pie. I've had two slices already, but I grab a spoon, cut a big chunk off the side of hers, and shove it into my mouth. Hope raises her fork and brings it down on the table with a *thunk*.

"Hey! I could've lost a finger," I protest.

"Next time you will. Get your own pie, mister."

"Yours tastes sooo much better."

"Grow up, Cato. You're twelve years old now."

"Almost thirteen."

Hope eats the last mouthful of pie and scrapes the plate with her fork. "Do you think Moses found a new home? Nobody could love him more than me."

I take off my Rangers cap and twirl it around on my finger. In my mind, I can still see that yellow ball of fur fighting for its next breath. He's not healed yet, although he's getting better. I'll fetch him from Mason's house in a few weeks when the scratches and burns will be gone...or at least not so bad.

Seeing Hope like this makes me sad, though. I wish I could tell her he's safe and taken care of. But then I'd have to tell her what happened to him.

"I miss my little kitty." Hope is staring at me now, her elbows on the table, chin resting in her hands. Her eyes sparkle with tears.

"Um, I've gotta go to practice." I stand up, pat Hope on the shoulder, and rush out the back door.

As I run, I force my thoughts to baseball. Baseball always makes sense to me.

The Rangers are waiting when I get to Walker Field, sitting underneath the sycamore tree, their backs against the trunk. With the schoolhouse on one side, the ball field on the other, and our sycamore in the middle, this place is like a second home. It's scrubby, though, compared to what the Marlins have, and I see that clear as day.

By now the Rangers know that Trace Blackburn lied on us. But one good thing is gonna come out of it: A whole day on shining, perfect Poplar Field.

Raymond D. rushes up to me and stabs a finger in my chest. "We ain't gonna practice with them lying dogs!"

I let out a long breath and push his finger away. "We don't have a choice, man. Not if we want to use that field."

"Yeah, but why did they lie?" asks Smokey Joe, our relief pitcher, for the hundredth time.

"Don't matter," says Mason.

"I still don't like it. Playing with the Marlins! Guys, we'll be like rats in a trap." Our center fielder, CP, claps his hands together, making a sound like a mousetrap closing. "I just know they'll do something sneaky."

"Y'all are being a bunch of sissies!" Our shortstop, Skeeter, always says things that nobody cares to hear. Eyes roll.

"I think we're lucky," says right-fielder Hank. "We're just gonna play a friendly game, nothing else. Somebody could've shot us last week. My uncle got buckshot for trespass once."

Everybody gets real quiet for a moment.

"Stop talking. Let's go," says left-fielder Monte. He gets up and takes off running, and the rest of us race after him.

We run in silence. Nothing left to say, I reckon.

I can't stop thinking about how strangely this season is starting out. 'Stead of the Rangers practicing on Walker Field with the Burgaw Barons—another Tidewater Colored League team—we're going to practice on one of the finest, neatest fields I have ever seen. Means we gotta fool around with a bunch of white boys, and I'm not happy about that, but still.

I just need to remember one thing: that sweet-potato-headed boy and his crew are nothing but trouble, so I gotta keep my wits about me.

The sides of my mouth turn down when I remember how sad Hope was this morning. Don't know how I'll be able to be around them, really... But then, like a flash of lightning, it comes to me.

"Time out, Rangers!" I yell, turning around and waving my arms in the air. Everyone stops running and gathers 'round me. "You know, fellas, we are gonna have some fun today."

"Fun?" says Raymond D., throwing his hands up in the air. "How're we gonna have fun with a bunch of fibbers and sneaks?"

"Shadow ball."

I wait for them to think about it. The Rangers look at one another. One by one they smile and nod.

"Man, that's a great idea," says Mason. "White boys don't know what shadow ball is. It'll be mighty funny watching them try to figure things out!"

"Those white boys will be scratching their heads 'til their hair falls out!" says Monte.

"It'll give 'em a taste of their own medicine, that's for sure. So, every-body in?" I ask.

"For sure!" says CP.

A bunch of *amens* and *you betchas* follow from the rest of the team. We all turn and start running toward Poplar Field. We're grinning this time.

Every colored player knows what shadow ball is. Lots of Negro League teams play it before the real game starts. The main thing about shadow ball is that it's played *without* a baseball, but the players are so good, people watching *think* there is one. (Isaac taught us how to play it a year ago. We've been having fun with it ever since.)

When we pass the white-barked poplar trees that mark the turn for Poplar Field, we race through the woods in a single line until we reach the clearing. Most of the Marlins are already on the field, practicing their throwing, fielding, and hitting.

Trace and Freight Train are standing near home plate. Spotting us, the rest of the Marlins run and huddle around the two of them. There's a bunch of whispering, then Trace turns to face us and the Marlins line up on both sides of him.

Now they're running toward us. Slowly at first, then faster, like a herd of buffalo.

Me and Mason look at one another. "What in the world are they doing?" he asks.

"I don't know, but we better get ready. Rangers! Line up. Tight!" I yell.

Rangers move quickly to form a line: shoulder to shoulder, ready to fight.

I take in a deep breath. The Marlins are running at full speed now. My heart pounds. I plant my feet steady on the ground and brace myself for the hit.

But just as they're about to crash into us, they stop. Inches away, each Marlin stamps his foot, turns quickly, and races back to home plate. There they throw their hands up and yell *"Marlins Number One!"* The whole team doubles over in laughter, pointing fingers at us.

"That was stupid," says Mason.

Heads nod. We all agree. But it's worse than stupid: They were trying to threaten us.

"They won't be laughing after they see what we've got for them," says Raymond D.

Trace and Freight Train walk up to me and Mason. Freight Train pokes his elbow into Trace's side, then glares at us.

"Daddy said he wanted us to practice with y'all," Trace says stiffly, "but he didn't say how long. Let's play a short game and get this over with."

Freight Train steps out in front of Trace. He looks even bigger than he did at the store last week. "It's a waste of time fooling with you colored boys. You ain't real baseball players anyways."

I move right in front of Freight Train, my hands resting on my hip bones, chest stuck out as far as it will go. "What do *you* know about colored baseball? The Rangers have been champions in the Tidewater Colored League for three years in a row."

"Colored league? Neega ball for neega boys!" says Freight Train, sneering. "You can't play in the big leagues, so it don't count." He looks at Trace and laughs again.

A rush of heat goes all through me. That word *again*! My hands ball into fists. Somebody needs to shut this boy up.

Mason steps up beside me. "You talk a lot. Let's see what you can do on the ball field, big mouth."

Whoa! Tell him, Mason.

Before anyone can say another word, Trace puts an arm between us and Freight Train. "Listen, the sooner we start, the sooner we can all go home. Marlins will be first at bat."

"What happened to flipping a coin?" asks Mason.

"We need to warm up first," I say to Trace.

He frowns. "You should've done that before you got here."

"Well, we're gonna do it now." I gesture to the Rangers to take their positions.

As I step onto the mound, I smile. Time for shadow ball!

First, we throw real balls around so the Marlins will think we're warming up. I toss the baseball back and forth to Mason in the catcher's spot, then I throw it to every player in position. Most of the Marlins stand at the edge of the field, talking amongst themselves, paying us no mind. But Freight Train sits on the bleachers, elbows on his knees, leaning forward, and Trace stands facing us, staring at me. Those two are watching more closely than anyone else, but I'm sure that neither one of them see when I make the baseball disappear.

My trick is simple. When Mason walks out to the mound to huddle with me, I bend down, pretending to tie my shoe—and slip the baseball inside my shirt that's tucked loosely in my pants.

Now the clowning and the fun begins.

Me and Mason pretend to toss the ball back and forth some more, this time moving lightning fast. On the fifth throw, Mason grabs his forehead, like he's been hit by the ball, and falls sideways. He lays there for a moment, then gets up, rushes out to the mound, yells at me, and pokes me lightly in the chest. We scuffle with one another until the rest of the team runs out to the mound.

"Boooooooo!"

"Get off the field!"

The Marlins yell at us from the sidelines. Trace paces back and forth. Freight Train pounds his fist into his open palm and stares.

We Rangers ignore them and return to our positions on the field, hiding smirks. Hank, our best batter, steps up to the plate, raises his bat, and waits for the pitch. I wind up and pretend to hurl the ball. We hear a *thump*. Sounds like it comes from Mason's glove, but no one seems to notice that it's our shortstop Skeeter who makes the sound!

I want to laugh so bad!

Hank lowers his bat for a moment, stares at Mason, then raises it in position for the next pitch. I wind up and pretend to throw another ball. Hank swings and we hear another *thump*! This time Hank lowers his bat and buries his head in his shoulder. He's trying not to laugh, I just know it.

Now every one of the Marlins is booing at us. I wind up and pretend to throw my last pitch. Hank swings, hard—Skeeter's special hand clap making the *crack* sound—then drops his bat and races toward first base. We Rangers strain our necks looking up at the sky, heads seeming to follow the path of the ball. Skeeter turns and runs full out looking up as if he sees it, holding his glove as if he aims to catch it on the fly.

I glance at the Marlins out of the corner of my eye. All heads are turned upward, trying to figure out where the ball is. Skeeter pretends to catch it, then throws the ball to first base where Raymond D pretends to tag Hank for an out. Afterward, he whips his arm in an overhand throw back to me on the pitcher's mound.

Two of the Marlins are not looking up at the sky like the rest of them. Freight Train stands on the side of the field, icy cold eyes fixed on me. Trace is bent forward beside him, both hands resting on his knees, shaking his head and muttering to himself.

Next thing I know, Trace straightens up and comes walking across the field—real fast, arms swinging back and forth with each step. Freight Train and the rest of the Marlins are right behind him.

*Uh-oh.*

Mason sees what's happening. With so many eyes on me, it's not safe to get the baseball that I hid in my shirt. He comes running, handing me a baseball out of his pocket, hoping to make it seem like we played with it. Then I turn to face the Marlins.

"Lemme see that ball!" Trace yells, sticking out his hand.

I put the baseball in the middle of his palm. He turns it slowly between his fingers, looking at every inch of it, then hands it to Freight Train, who does the same, shrugs, and hands the ball back to Trace.

"Don't know what you did to this baseball, but it was *something*," says Trace. His cheeks are red and he's breathing hard. He takes a step toward me, closer than he ought to. "Marlins don't play with cheaters. You hear me?"

"You boys are asking for a whuppin'," growls Freight Train.

"*Uh-huh!*" the Marlins players say all together.

"That's enough! Let's just play some ball and go home," says Trace. He heads to the sidelines to get his glove.

"No! We are not gonna play with no cheaters." Freight Train crosses his arms over his chest and stands still. The rest of the Marlins do the same.

"Liar! Rangers do not cheat!" I yell.

"Balls-o-fire! That's the second time you called me a liar. I can't let you get away with that, neega!" Freight Train raises his arms, ready to fight.

Before Mason can hold me back, I rush at Freight Train and crash into him with all my weight.

I was intending to shove him to the ground. But it's like hitting a wall of rock.

Freight Train grins a gap-toothed grin, pushes me to the ground, and slams himself on top of me. His big shoulders pin me down, crushing me. Then he turns so that he's sitting on my chest, and starts hitting me about the head with his huge fists. All I feel is pain.

There are bodies all around, now. Two or three Rangers have jumped on Freight Train's back and are trying to pull him off of me. Everybody's fighting. I'm on the bottom of a pile of boys, hemmed in. I can't breathe.

Striking with my elbows and kicking with my feet, I fight free and try to stand—but a hand catches hold of my shirt and pulls me back into the pile. I swing wildly, hoping my fists smash into anyone with white skin. Rangers and Marlins are wrapped around one another in a sweaty, tangled mess. Then—

*Kapow!*

My heart stops. Everybody goes still, as if we were just doused with cold water.

Slowly, Rangers and Marlins untangle themselves, stagger up, and look around.

"Fight's over!" Mr. Luke Blackburn is standing on the back of his pickup truck, shotgun raised high, pointing at the sky. "Don't want to see another fist raised."

A hush comes over us.

Mr. Luke lowers the shotgun. "You boys are a disgrace to the game of baseball."

Silence. Most all of us look down at the ground.

"I thought you boys could at least *practice* on your own. I was wrong. I reckon you need some grown folks to watch you."

Mr. Luke jumps off the back of the pickup truck and walks toward us. In silence, he looks each one of us in the face, striding back and forth before the group of boys.

"*Trace! Cato!* Stand in front," he yells. We hop to it, the same expression on both our faces: eyes wide, lips tight. "Well now. Maybe you boys didn't understand me before. I'm gonna talk real slow and real quiet now, and the two of you better break your necks listening. *Or else.*

"You've got a problem, boys, and the two of you are going to solve it. A man's word is his bond. You agreed to play a practice game against one another. Can't trust you to do that, it seems, but I won't let you weasel out of that agreement. As team captains, what are you gonna do to fulfill your pledge?"

Me and Trace are still wide-eyed, chewing on our bottom lips. I can feel the tips of my ears burning; Trace's cheeks and forehead are pink as can be. If he's like me, he's wondering what the rest of the team is thinking, watching this. We're so far in front, they can't hear what Mr. Luke is saying, but they can see us being shamed.

Mr. Luke looks back and forth between me and Trace. "Speak up, boys. I can't hear you. How are you gonna keep your word to play together?"

For a moment, all I hear is June Bugs chirping in the grass. And then a curious thing happens. The Tidewater Colored League championship spirit rises up in me, and I think I know the answer. What I say next surprises even my own self.

59

"Mr. Luke? We could have a bona fide baseball game between the Rangers and the Marlins."

Even before I turn my head to look at him, I just know Trace is 'bout to bust. "New Hanover Marlins been regional champions the past three years now," he says stiffly. "If you think your raggedy little team of colored boys can beat us, you is bona fide *crazy*." His eyes narrow.

Mr. Luke lays his hand gently on hisshoulder. "Ain't nobody crazy here, Trace. Rangers are champions in their own league, just like you are in yours. I never talked about this, Lord knows I should have, but there are teams of colored players in the Negro Baseball Leagues that are really, really fine. Some of them are much better than a lot of white teams! Why, Cato's daddy Moses was one of the best baseball players to come out of Carolina—ever. He played with the Kansas City Monarchs out in Missouri. Wouldn't be surprised if Cato wasn't just as good as his daddy. So, if you think the Marlins are better than the Rangers, you'll have to prove it."

Me and Trace glare at one another.

"It's settled then," says Mr. Luke. "Two weeks from today, the New Hanover Marlins will play the Pender County Rangers right here at Poplar Field. A real match. It's a mighty fine idea, Cato—a good way to clear the air and have an honest contest. That'll build respect between you boys. Now go and tell your teammates."

"This is kind of crazy, Daddy," mutters Trace.

"No, son. It's not crazy. It's baseball."

The Rangers and Marlins each gather in huddles as me and Trace explain what Mr. Luke has just made us agree to. Seems every guy on the field hangs his head and groans loudly at the same time.

"Boys!" Mr. Luke loudly calls us all to attention. We stand and face him—and then he looks right at me. "Tell your grandpa to spread the word! Colored folks are invited to walk through the front gate and sit on the bleachers like everybody else."

"Yes suh," I say, my voice so soft nobody hears me.

Then Mr. Luke looks straight at Trace and his teammates. "Marlins! Tell your people that this is going to be one of the best games they've ever seen!"

They just stare at him in shock.

"That's all for now, boys. You can go home." Mr. Luke waves his hand in the air like he's shooing chickens.

Still staring, nobody moves.

"*Git!*" he yells.

We all scatter. Marlins head for the pickup trucks they came in. Rangers head toward the narrow path that leads back to the main road and home. We run in silence at a slow trot. Not even Skeeter has a word to say.

My head is spinning. I can't believe what just happened.

A bona fide baseball game with the Marlins. I'm wondering, now, if this is a good idea. Sure, we'll beat the snot out of them and get bragging rights, but they're not in the Tidewater Colored League, so it won't help us win another championship. And it's gonna take time away from our practices.

Man! All this trouble just from wanting to see a new baseball field!

*Out of the frying pan and into the fire* is what Gran would say. For the first time, I know what that saying truly means.

# Chapter 10
## STRIKE ONE

Sunday supper is for family. We're all seated at the kitchen table, ready to eat the fried chicken, succotash, okra, rice, and cornbread that Gran cooked today.

"Sit down and say the blessing, Amos," says Papa Vee as Rev rushes in at the last moment. "Everybody's hungry."

"Sorry I'm late, folks." Rev starts the prayer before any of us can even shut our eyes.

"Amen," we all say when grace is over.

"Thank you, son." Gran stares hard at Rev. There are tears in her eyes. "I'm always touched by the way you say that grace...the sound of your voice, the words I heard my granddaddy say for so many years..." She looks at Hope and me. "Teach it to your children and my granddaddy will live forever."

"Yes'm," me and Hope say.

"Just give me a little bit of everything, Mama J," says Rev, eyeing every dish on the table. Gran takes a plate and piles it high with what looks like two servings of each dish. I frown, hoping there's some left for the rest of us.

Though we don't say it out loud, me and Rev race to see which one of us can eat the most at Sunday supper, just like me and Daddy Mo used to do.

"What's this I hear about a match between the Rangers and the Marlins?" asks Rev, his mouth full.

"Amos, be an example for the children," says Gran, pointing at her mouth.

"Yes'm," says Rev.

I lower my head and shove a forkful of food into my mouth. The last thing I want to talk about is that game.

"Well, near as I can tell, Amos," says Papa Vee, eyeing me, "Cato and the Rangers just had to see Luke's new ball field. They snuck over there, somebody saw them and told Luke about it, and the rest, well...the rest seems as tangled as a fly in a spider's web. There was some trouble between the boys, and they've decided to settle things with a match."

I cut my eyes at him.

"Mercy! Thought Luke Blackburn didn't know a thing about Cato." Rev reaches for another square of cornbread.

"He does now. Saw him up close when the Rangers went into Luke's store the other day." Papa Vee glances at me. My mouth goes dry and I have trouble swallowing. Did I cause all this trouble? It was my idea to see Poplar Field.

"Well, if I know Luke, he would've wanted to punish the Rangers real good for trespassing on his fancy ball field," mutters Rev.

"Cato and Mason only had to do some chores at Luke's store. That's not much punishment," says Gran.

"He told them to ask next time," Papa Vee goes on. "You know, when Cato and I went to see Luke last week, seeing us made him think about the old days..."

"The old days?" Rev leans forward, a low fire growing in his eyes. "Which one? Maybe the day that I lost my brother? The day that Isaac, Cato, and Hope lost their daddy—and you and Mama J lost your son—all on account of Luke Blackburn?"

"*Amos!*" Gran gives Rev a look that could melt iron.

He sits back in his chair. His shoulders slump. "Mo and me grew up together in this very house. I miss him every day, and I don't know if I'll ever forgive Luke Blackburn for taking him away from us."

Gran pats Rev's arm. "Amos, it's not fair to say it was him. A whole lot of people did things. Besides—" Gran looks from Rev to me to Hope, "you've said too much already."

Rev holds his head down and stares at his plate. Me and Hope look at one another. We've never seen Rev get mad like that. We've never heard him talk like this in front of us.

What does he mean, *On account of Luke Blackburn*? Sweat slides down my back.

"The game is in two weeks, Amos, on Luke's new ball field in New Hanover," says Papa Vee mildly. "Now that's enough about Luke Blackburn. Pass the chicken, please."

We continue eating, with Gran chattering on about the gossip she heard at her sewing circle. The rest of us scrape our forks over our plates and chew.

"Anybody got room for pie?" asks Gran when she sees we're all done eating.

"Always got room for pie, Mama J," says Rev, smiling now.

Gran waves at me. "Go outside and get those apple pies cooling on the porch, Cato."

"Yes'm," I say.

But as soon as I get up from the table, I see a boy pass the window in a blur and run up on the porch. He pounds furiously on the door.

"*Mr. Vernon! Miss Nina! Let me in!*"

"That's Harlee Junior!" says Hope, sitting up in her chair.

Rev jumps up first, Papa Vee right behind him. He opens the door. It *is* Harlee Junior.

"Harlee? Come on in," says Rev. "Goodness gracious, what happened to you, son?"

Harlee Jamison Junior's shirt is torn to pieces. There're scratches on his neck and arms, and a cut underneath his left eye. A few drops of blood trickle down the side of his mouth. We all crowd around him, Hope wiggling her way in front of everybody.

"They was planning—to defile the church, Rev—throw paint on it or—write something bad!" Harlee Junior is out of breath and talking so fast we can barely keep up with what he's saying.

"Slow down, son. Who was going to defile the church?" asks Rev calmly.

"Three white boys! They was wearing red T-shirts, and they had red kerchiefs tied on their faces. When they saw me, they dropped the brushes and paint cans they was holding and started running after me. Caught me, too—threw me on the ground and kicked me a few times." Harlee Junior glances at Hope when he says this. Her eyes go soft, and she takes a step closer to him. "Somehow I got back on my feet and outrunned them."

Gran disappears onto the back porch and returns a moment later. "Move over, Amos. I need to see about this boy." She steps in front of everybody and dabs at the cuts on his face with a damp white cloth. Harlee Junior and Hope keep looking at one another.

"Hmm," says Papa Vee. "White boys coming into a colored town means trouble."

"We'd better go over to the church and see what's going on," says Rev, heading outside. Papa Vee follows close behind him—and Harlee Junior, who rushes after them both.

"Gran, can I go too?" I bolt out the door before she can answer. I'm old enough to see.

Rev's pickup truck is already driving out of the yard. I run and jump on the back with Harlee Junior. Hope is standing on the porch, waving. Harlee Junior smiles and waves back—but pulls his arm down real fast when he sees me looking at him.

Saint John's Church is less than a mile from our house. When we're about halfway there, we hear voices—yelling and name-calling. I lean over the side of the truck to get a better look.

Six or seven boys, white and colored alike, are in the middle of the road—fighting!

The white boys are wearing red T-shirts and red kerchiefs around their necks, just like Harlee said. Why? Is it a disguise?

Rev starts blowing the horn. When that doesn't stop anything, he aims the truck toward the middle of the pack, honking louder, and presses the gas. He's only feet away before the boys look up, break apart, and jump out of the way. While the colored boys brush themselves off, the white boys scatter into the woods.

Me and Harlee Junior jump off the truck and take off running after them. We don't think about it—we just do it. But by the time we catch up, all we see is a green pickup truck speeding off, flinging red mud. There are three white boys on the back of it, pointing their fingers at us and laughing.

"Dang it!" Harlee Junior yells.

Panting, we walk back to Rev's pickup truck. I think about the faces I just saw . . . or parts of faces. Some of the boys seemed pretty young, but the bigger ones—the ones that beat up Harlee Junior, I reckon—were prob'ly older, 'bout my age. Wonder why all of those boys were wearing red?

"You fellas are a natural mess," says Rev. He's talking to three colored boys sitting on the back of his truck, the ones that were fighting. They wear baseball caps—gray ones—for the Burgaw Barons.

Harlee Junior runs up to one of them and raises his hand, but the boy pushes his arm away. "I'm all right, Harlee—I ain't no baby!"

"Yeah? What's Daddy gonna say when he sees you, Buster Boy?" Harlee Junior holds his young brother still to get a better look at the scratch on his forehead.

"Hey, the white boys got hurt too," says Buster Boy proudly.

"We didn't start it!" insists another boy. "We was just walking home from baseball practice and they jumped us." He's been hit hard in the mouth, and his lips are starting to swell. The boy next to him is worse—he has a bloody nose.

"Come on, fellas," says Rev. "We need to get you cleaned up before your mamas see you."

The ride back home seems longer than when we came. We boys all sit quiet on the back of the truck, staring past one another. Everybody's got cuts and bruises but me. I blow out a long breath. Lordy. I wish we'd caught those white boys and I'd whupped them just a little bit.

Gran and Hope are sitting on the front porch swing when we drive into the yard. The truck stops and the boys get off and walk toward the house.

"Land's sake, Amos! What's happened now?"

"Boys fighting, Mama J.," says Rev, leaning out the window of the truck. "They say some white boys jumped them. We never got to the church—take care of the children while Papa Vee and I go to have a look."

"All right, Amos."

Gran marches the boys into the kitchen where she and Hope wash their cuts with soap and water and put iodine on them. The boys are all smiles after that, mostly on account of the big slices of apple pie that Gran gives them.

Harlee Junior and Hope are eating theirs while making eyes at one another. I'm gonna have to give that girl a talking-to.

When Gran offers me a piece, I shake my head. I'm not hungry, not even for apple pie. All I can think about is what Harlee Junior said, and what I saw: white boys coming around to defile a colored church; white boys fighting colored boys; white boys in red shirts and red kerchiefs.

It was like they were in a club. I've a feeling that means something. But what?

# Chapter 11

## FOUL TERRITORY

This baseball season is starting out all wrong.

Strange things keep happening. The match between the Rangers and the Marlins. The fight between the white and colored boys in Burgaw. The spilled paint Rev and Papa Vee found in the churchyard. Can't wait 'til everything is settled down.

"Get up, sleepyhead!" Hope yanks the pantry curtain back and hits me in the face with a wet rag. "We're leaving for church soon. You'd better hurry and get dressed."

I pull the covers up over my head.

"I *know* you heard me." The tone of Hope's voice tells me she's got one hand on her hip, just like Gran.

"Yeah," I say, throwing off the covers suddenly and showing my underwear.

Hope gags and closes the curtain in a hurry, but keeps talking. "We've got people coming to Saint John's from Spivey's Corner this Sunday. Maybe you'll see your sweetheart, Joanne!"

"Girl, you need to stop talking about Joanne."

"Never!" says Hope, giggling.

"Then just stop talking." I get up and pull the curtain back just enough to throw a dirty sock at her.

"Missed me!" she yells as she darts off.

Dang it.

Truthfully, church is the last place I want to go today, but when the preacher is in the family, that's what you do—go every Sunday, and sometimes during the week. I'd rather hunt for the white boys that beat up Harlee Junior. Me and the Rangers would give them the whuppin' of their lives. We'd teach them not to mess with colored boys from Pender County.

I get up, walk through the kitchen out to the back porch, and pump some water in a basin. Then I carry it back into the pantry and give myself a bird bath. I put on my Sunday pants, a white shirt, and a blue tie that once belonged to Daddy Mo. It's long, so after I tie a knot, I tuck it into the waist of my pants.

There's food after church, so no proper breakfast this morning. I grab two cold biscuits from the pan on the stove, slap some fatback in between, and head out the door. Gran and Hope and Papa Vee are already sitting in the pickup truck, waiting for me. I hop onto the back and eat my biscuits.

By the time we get to church, everybody's in their seats. We walk to our family spot in the front row and sit down as the congregation is singing the opening hymn. When they're done, Rev walks into the pulpit looking tall and powerful, like he always does during service.

Can't help but smile, remembering how Gran scolded him at supper.

Rev opens his Bible and reads the scripture, sounding the words out slowly and waiting for the congregation to repeat what he says. Gran and Papa Vee can read, but lots of folks in Sycamore Grove never went to school or learned their letters. So we use call-and-response in church, like colored folks have for a very long time.

After the scripture, Rev starts his sermon. "Today, Church, I'm going to talk about courage and faith."

I slump way down in my seat.

He talks. And talks. My eyes are heavy and starting to cross. Rev's voice seems far away, so I close my eyes...*Ahh*. Holy naps are the best kind. I always dream about baseball. Sometimes I'm pitching for the Kansas City Monarchs in the Negro World Series. Other times, me and Isaac are on the field getting pitching lessons from Satchel Paige...

"*Umph!*" I sit straight up in my seat. Gran just poked me so hard I felt a knife-sharp pain in my side. Hope covers her mouth with her hand and snickers. Across the aisle, four of the Rangers bury their mouths in their shirtsleeves, laughing. I raise my head, wide-awake now.

Rev is at the top of his sermon now, strutting back and forth in the pulpit, raising his arms in the air.

"And so, Church, the Master has a word for us today, from Matthew 5, verse 39. 'But I say unto you…whosoever shall smite thee on thy right cheek, turn to him the other also.' It takes courage to be patient with things that happen in this world, Church. And you've got to have faith that God will work it out for you. This is a message I want everyone to hear this morning, especially the young'uns, especially our boys."

I sit up straighter in my seat now.

"Church, there's mischief afoot in Pender County—fights amongst young white and colored boys, folks planning to desecrate the church. Can't say what it's all about, but it's not a good thing. We need to be careful lest we find ourselves faced with trouble we could do without.

"Now, I know how you young boys feel. It's natural to want to defend yourselves if somebody starts a fight; seems cowardly and unmanly if you don't. But some fights are more trouble than they're worth. Even if you win, you lose. The fellas in Burgaw were jumped by mischievous white boys—following up on a dare, probably. Jumping on colored boys is part of growing up for a white boy in the South. We don't want our boys, especially the Rangers, getting mixed up in any of this; don't want older white boys to have an excuse to come into our community talking 'bout defending their little brothers. Next thing you know, there'll be grown folks involved. Then we've really got trouble on our hands.

"Now we know the Rangers are supposed to play a ball game against the white boys from New Hanover in a week. That might be the reason for all of this mess, or it might not, but I want you to keep a cool head, boys. And remember, this is just one game in a lifetime of playing baseball. When it's over, things will be just the way they were before, unless…"

Rev's voice gets louder now.

"...Unless you do something foolish that changes everything." He looks around the church, his eyes falling on baseball players wherever we sit.

A soft "amen" rises from the congregation.

"Young men, save your anger and your energy for baseball. Be smart. Stay strong and healthy—so you can beat the living daylights out of those New Hanover boys. Praise the Lord!"

"*Praise the Lord!*" the congregation calls out, leaping to their feet and clapping loudly.

But I can't stand with them. And I certainly can't cheer. My stomach is in knots. Rev just reminded us to turn the other cheek, but does that mean I have to slink away from fights like a coward? Let white boys beat the snot out of us if they want to?

I rise for the benediction, then sit back down. Everyone rushes out the door to the Sunday dinner set up in the churchyard, but I'm not hungry. I want to get even; I want to make things right, somehow. 'Cause they feel very wrong to me now.

As everyone goes outside, Rangers mill around at the front of the church talking amongst themselves. It's not long before they gather at the pew I'm sitting on, staring into my face.

"Rev don't really mean it, not deep in his heart," says Skeeter. "He can't mean for us to let somebody beat on us and do nothing about it."

"He's a preacher," says Mason. "He means it."

"So, fine, we won't go looking for them. But what're we gonna do if those white boys jump somebody else, Cato?" asks Raymond D.—the one most likely to want to fight, besides me.

I let out a long breath, get up without saying a word to anybody, and walk outside.

"Cato? Where you goin', man?" Skeeter calls after me.

The churchyard is full of children playing and grown folks talking and laughing. We've got company from the congregation at Spivey's Corner, so there's twice as many folks as most Sundays. Mason's cousin Joanne is standing near Gran, but I walk the other way.

Hope sees me and rushes over. "Your girlfriend is here," she says, laughing.

I frown.

"Uh-oh," says Hope. "You look mad. It's because of what Rev said, isn't it? But I'm sure it's okay to fight back if somebody else starts it and they're getting the best of you. Gran and Papa Vee taught us to stand up for ourselves."

"All I know is, if a white boy starts a fight, won't be no pondering. I plan to knock him into next week."

"Well, just be careful. I don't want you or anybody else to get hurt."

"If we get hurt, Gran will patch us up."

"And me," says Hope. "But we can't work miracles!"

All a sudden, she gets a strange look on her face. Her forehead creases. She hugs herself as if she's freezing, and looks up at the sky.

"What's the matter?" I ask.

"I just felt a really cold wind blow over me. Gran says that's a sign of something, I don't remember what."

At the same time, me and Hope turn around and search the churchyard to see where Gran is now. She's standing at the table closest to the road, arms crossed over her chest, shaking her head and staring into the distance.

"Something's wrong," I say.

Hope nods, and we rush across the churchyard until we reach Gran's side. By now, other people are staring in the same direction as Gran.

Now I see what Gran sees…a man walking toward the church, carrying something.

His steps are slow and unsteady. He's wearing a green Army jacket, black boots, and a baseball cap: gray-and-black striped, with an *M* for the Kansas City Monarchs. I would know a hat like that anywhere.

"Who's coming up the road, Vee?" asks Gran. "What's he carrying?"

Before Papa Vee can answer her, Gran starts out to meet the stranger, walking slowly at first, then faster and faster.

"Nina, wait!" calls Papa Vee, following her.

But Gran ain't waiting. She screams *"Lord a mercy!"* and takes off running, fast for a woman her age. I set out like a bullet running after her. As I get closer, I see that the stranger has something slung over his shoulder—almost like a prize deer from hunting. But it's not a deer. It's...

It's a man.

His arms are dangling down the stranger's back. The stranger grips the man's legs tight around the thighs, just below his bottom.

Gran falls to her knees and buries her face in her hands. *"Isaac!"* she screams. Her voice cuts through the air like a knife. "Oh God! Isaac!"

# Chapter 12
## HEALING HANDS

Me and Papa Vee watch in silence as the stranger reaches us, every step he takes heavy, like a man walking through mud. His cap is pulled low over his eyes. His jacket and trousers are spotted with blood.

Gran is still kneeling, hugging herself and rocking back and forth. Tears pour down her face and onto the front of her Sunday dress. Together, me and Papa Vee gently lift her to her feet.

The stranger looks at Gran. "He's alive, ma'am. Just want you to know that."

"Thank God!" Gran slumps into Papa Vee's arms.

I close my eyes, breathe out a long breath, and say a prayer of thanks. Hope comes up behind me and folds her arms around me. I turn and put my arm around her shoulder.

Now the congregation rushes up to the stranger, swarming around him like bees. Rev steps forward, his arms outstretched. "Son, let me—"

"No!" The stranger steps back suddenly.

Rev looks at Gran. She wipes her face with her apron, then reaches out with a trembling hand. "Isaac is my grandson. Let's take my boy home."

Everyone follows as Gran starts walking to our pickup, her long apron swirling with each step: first the stranger, then Rev and Papa Vee, then me and Hope and the rest.

"Cato!" Gran calls and I run to her side. "Run on ahead of us. It'll take some time to load your brother on the truck and get him comfortable. Tell Nate and Ollie I'll need things extra clean—they'll know what to do. Then look in my cedar chest and get fresh sheets. Tear them into strips."

"Me too, Gran?" asks Hope. "Should I run ahead too?"

"No, child. Stay close to me. You're my right hand today."

Before I even look for him, Mason is right beside me. "Rangers are here, man," he says.

I nod, and me and the Rangers run toward home, our feet pounding the road. When we get there, I call out to Nate and Ollie: "*Isaac's home and he's hurt bad!*"

"Lawd! What happened?" asks Ollie.

"We'll find out soon enough," says Nate. "What Miss Nina want us to do?"

"Make things extra clean is what she said."

"We've done that plenty times," says Ollie. I realize I've seen them do this once before: I was there when Gran helped Miss Ruby birth her last baby.

"Gon' be some blood, I reckon. Come on!" Nate grabs Ollie by the arm and they head inside.

I remember what else I'm 'sposed to do and why. Me and Mason fetch sheets from the cedar chest and start ripping them into strips. Gran and the healers will use the pieces I tear to clean dirt from Isaac's wounds—that'll help them to heal faster and keep from festering, poisoning Isaac's blood. That's a lesson I learned because Gran is a healer.

Before we're half done, Gran and Hope burst into the kitchen. "Stand aside, boys. I need to get things ready before they bring Isaac in."

Gran moves quickly. She sweeps a hand across the kitchen table that Nate and Ollie cleaned, just to make sure it's dry. Then she takes two full sheets Hope hands her and spreads them over the tabletop.

"Cato, get two more sheets and lay them on top of these. Then get a pillow from my bed to put under Isaac's head."

"Yes'm," I say, but before I leave the room, I silently point to the things on the floor and Mason picks them up.

When I get back to the kitchen, I see the stranger on the porch, looking through the screen door with Isaac on his back again. Rev and Papa Vee are standing next to him. The Rangers and the rest of the church folks are crowded behind them.

Gran opens the screen door to let the stranger in. He steps into the kitchen, bending low to keep Isaac from hitting the doorframe. His Monarchs baseball cap falls off, revealing thick black hair and smooth Karo-syrup-brown skin. He's younger than he seemed at first. It's the dark circles under his eyes that made him look old.

"God bless you for bringing my son home," says Gran.

"Yes, ma'am."

Papa Vee, Rev, and a few of the church deacons crowd into the kitchen now. Miss Mary Agnes and Miss Naomi, Gran's lifelong friends and fellow healers, push their way up next to her. Hope stays close to her, too.

The stranger takes a step toward the table, then stops. His brown eyes dart around the room, landing on first one face and then another. Rev and Papa Vee reach out to him, but he pulls away. Gran lays her hand gently on his arm.

"You can let go now, son. Isaac's home and we'll take good care of him."

The stranger looks at Gran with tears in his eyes, but still does not move.

"What's your name, son?" asks Gran.

"My name is Daniel, ma'am."

"Let us help you, Daniel." She nods toward Rev, Papa Vee, and the church deacons.

The stranger loosens his hold on Isaac. Slowly, carefully, the men peel Isaac from the stranger's grip and lay him on the kitchen table. Folks standing on the porch push closer and stare through the screen, mumbling amongst themselves:

"Have mercy!"

"Oh my Lord!"

Isaac's face is caked with dried blood, his eyes are swollen shut, and his lower lip is busted open. Blood dribbles from a cut on one side of his forehead, running down his temple and onto his neck. He doesn't look like himself at all.

I close my eyes and take in a deep breath. Lordy.

*Who did this to my brother?*

The stranger wipes his face with the blood-stained sleeve of his jacket and steps away.Hope leans over Isaac, looking into his face. She covers her mouth with one hand and shakes her head slowly. Tears roll down her cheeks. I bite down hard on my lower lip, holding back tears, but when I look up at Rev and Papa Vee I see tears in their eyes too. Hope wipes her eyes and fetches Gran's powders from the cabinet.

Isaac's legs dangle over the edge of the table. Rev lifts his feet and holds them in his hands. A message ripples through the crowd and two crates are brought in to prop them up.

I stand by Isaac's head and look him over closely, head to toe. His pants are torn, one knee bloody; his favorite shirt, the striped blue and white one that belonged to Daddy Mo, is in tatters. But his chest is moving up and down, and I say a prayer of thanks for that.

The coppery scent of dried blood hangs in the air, drifting up my nose and tickling the back of my throat, making me gag. This smell belongs to the outdoors—to November, when the Pender County men kill hogs, cut up the meat, and hang it in smokehouses to keep for winter. Now the stench of butchering is in Gran's kitchen, where the smell of hot molasses biscuits—the smell of love—is all I've ever known.

I press against my stomach with my fist to keep from throwing up. I bite the inside of my cheek, too, until the sweet taste of blood fills my mouth. Gran must sense that I'm struggling. While Miss Mary Agnes and Miss Naomi begin undressing Isaac, she quickly walks behind me, puts her hand on my back, and rubs circles, the way she used to when I was younger; the way she did the day we put Daddy Mo in the ground.

"Amos, we need a prayer, son," says Papa Vee.

A hush comes over the crowd. We bow our heads and join hands in a chain that goes all around the kitchen, out the back door, onto the porch, and into the yard.

Rev's voice is loud and strong so all can hear. "We thank you, Lord, for sparing the life of our son, Isaac Jones, and we ask that you make him strong again, Lord, strong enough to fulfill the destiny that you wrote for him on the day he was born. And we ask you to anoint the hands of your healers, Mama J, Miss Mary Agnes, Miss Naomi, and little Hope. Through them, touch the body of Isaac Jones and make him whole again. These things we ask in the name of the Father, the Son, and the Holy Spirit, amen."

"Amen," we say all together.

"All right now, clear out this kitchen and let us do God's work." Gran waves a hand in the air, and Papa Vee, Rev, and the deacons go outside, nudging the stranger along with them. Mr. D. K. Johnson, the builder, pushes against the tide, slips into the kitchen, and stands next to Gran. He leans close and whispers in her ear, then shoves a spool into her hand. Looks like fishing line to me. Just as quickly, he slips outside again.

What happens next is a flurry.

Me and Mason make sure that Gran and the healers have all the cloth they need. Nate and Ollie have started a campfire out back, so we can make sheets extra clean, the way Gran wants. First, we dunk sheets in boiling water, fish them out with a stick, put them in a washtub to cool, then take them to the kitchen for the healers to use. Bloody bandages are thrown into a bucket, and me and Mason take them back to the campfire. There we dunk them, one after the other, into washtubs filled with vinegar and water, then soap, then clear water. Now free of blood stains, the cloths are dunked into boiling water again and carried back to the kitchen.

Soon CP takes my place as a washer and runner, and I stand with the others on the back porch, my nose pressed against the screen door, watching. Before long, the dried blood is gone and Isaac's beautiful tan skin shines through. But that cut on his forehead won't stop bleeding.

Gran and the healers gather 'round, leaning over him. Then they all stand in a huddle in the corner of the room, whispering amongst themselves. Hope disappears into the back of the house and comes back with

Gran's sewing basket. I know what they're 'bout to do now. Moses wasn't the first cat Hope took in. Once, she had a gray kitten with a deep cut on the top of its head. Gran and Hope cleaned the wound, then took turns making stitches as they sewed it up with an embroidery needle and thread.

What they do next is more of making things extra clean. They take out a long needle and run it through the flame of a match; they dip a length of fishing line into a bowl of alcohol. I shut my eyes tight. This ain't no kitty. It's Isaac!

But I watch in wonder as my brave little sister pulls back in fear at first, then dips her hands in alcohol, dries them on a cloth, picks up the needle, and threads it with the fishing line that Gran hands to her.

"Don't get spooked if you hear him moan, child," says Gran.

Hope stops for just a moment, sweat gleaming on her forehead and upper lip, then she pushes the needle slowly, carefully, into our brother's skin. Sure enough, a low groan rises from Isaac's chest. Tears form in Hope's eyes, but she blinks them away and pushes the needle through one more time.

Lordy! I can't watch anymore! I back away from the screen door, bumping into people standing behind me on the porch.

I walk down the steps slowly. When I get on the ground and free of people, I tear out running across the yard and through the field on the side of the house. My heart pounds. Sweat pours down my face and back. But I don't stop running 'til I'm in the woods by the creek where me and Isaac used to play.

When I'm sure that no one can see me from the house, I drop to my knees, put my hands over my face, and let the tears pour down my cheeks. I rock back and forth, heaving. Then everything I've eaten all day spills out of my mouth and onto the ground. I think I'm done, but my body disagrees, and vomit flows—once, twice, three times. When it's over, I close my eyes and breathe deeply, nearly gagging from the stench.

Exhausted, I rest my butt on my heels and wipe my mouth with my shirtsleeve.

I'm scared.

# Chapter 13
## PHILLY DAN

My stomach has settled and the tears have stopped...for now. I'd better go back and see how Isaac is doing. But just as I start to get up, I hear a branch crack behind me. *Did somebody see me puke?*

I whirl around—and look right into the stranger's face.

"You all right, li'l brother?" he asks.

I draw in a breath, too surprised to answer.

"Bet your mouth tastes pretty bad. I've got something to fix that." The stranger reaches into the pocket of his blood-stained jacket and pulls out a small whiskey bottle.

"No!" I put my hand up to my mouth. "Gran won't allow drinking."

"You're too young anyhow. Sorry! I never had a day like this one." The stranger turns the whiskey bottle up to his mouth, empties it, and hurls it into the woods. "No disrespect to your grandma, but I needed that drink."

I stare at him for a moment, then walk over to the creek, kneel down, and splash my face with cool water. When I scoop up a handful to take a drink, the stranger comes over, lies flat on the ground, and sucks water into his mouth, loudly. He sounds like a pig. Another time I would laugh, but funny doesn't fit this day.

"Much better than whiskey." The stranger wipes his mouth with the filthy sleeve of his jacket. He takes another noisy drink, then sits on the ground beside me. "I need your help, li'l brother."

Gran taught me good manners, but I don't feel like being polite right now. So I don't answer him.

"Isaac and me both had satchels. I hid them behind a bush so no one would steal them, but I don't know how to get back to where we were. Don't know this country at all,. Will you help me?"

Lordy, no! I don't want to go there—don't want to see where Isaac's blood was spilt. I push against my stomach with my fist to keep from getting sick again.

"I understand how you might be feelin', but I can't find those bags by myself." The stranger's eyes are pleading.

As much as I don't want to take him, I can't let Isaac lose his things. "I'll go with you." Then I draw in a deep, shaky breath.

Me and the stranger walk back through the field, but as the house comes into sight, we turn and head out to the road. Folks are still milling around on the porch and in the yard. The crowd is smaller now—lots of people have prob'ly gone home. The Rangers, Papa Vee, Rev, Nate, Ollie, and some of the deacons are still standing around the campfires in the backyard. Mason sees us and waves. I wave back.

Me and the stranger walk along in silence until we get to Saint John's Church. Then we turn down the road the stranger walked, the one that leads away from Pender County and toward New Hanover County.

"What's your name again?" I ask.

"Daniel, but everybody calls me Philly Dan."

"How come?"

"When I joined the Monarchs, there was another fella name of Dan, so they started calling me Danny. Well, I don't look like no 'Danny'; don't feel like no 'Danny.' Grew up in Philadelphia, so I told them to call me Philly Dan."

I don't look at Philly Dan, nor do I say a word. After a while, he asks, "So how did you get your name? Was your granddaddy or somebody else in your family named Cato?"

"Papa Vee's my granddaddy. His name is Vernon. My daddy named me for a colored baseball player who lived a long time ago."

"Octavius Valentine Catto," says Philly Dan. "I know about him—he's from my hometown."

"My daddy was Moses Valentine Jones. He was sort of named for him too. But we called him Daddy Mo." Now I'm curious. "Didn't Isaac tell you about us?"

"Yeah! A lot. I knew your name—didn't I? See, Isaac and me are more than teammates. We're brothers. We eat together, sit together on the bus when the team travels, bunk together in the same room."

I take a long look at Philly Dan. His pants and his shirt are wrinkled, and his shoes are dirty, but they look big-city fine to me. Prob'ly cost a lot of money. He's good-looking too. Somehow I can't imagine my plain old brother being best friends with a fella like this.

"And where were you when Isaac got hurt?" I ask, surprising my own self.

Philly Dan's eyes narrow to tiny slits. He doesn't answer me, just walks faster, leaving me behind.

When I catch up to him, I ask again, "Where were you?"

After a sigh, he says, "I missed the bus that Isaac was on and had to take the next one."

"So Isaac was all by himself." My eyes keep darting sideways, looking at Philly Dan, trying to figure what kind of man he is. Then I think about Isaac and get scared all over again. I see him lying on the kitchen table, Gran, Hope, and the healers cleaning blood off every inch of him. I feel that rush of heat that comes just before I get really mad.

"None of this would've happened if you had been with him," I say, much louder now, hardly believing that I'm talking this way to someone so much older than me.

Philly Dan looks straight ahead and doesn't say anything.

"Maybe you didn't miss the bus. Maybe you were hiding in the bushes while Isaac was beat up." My voice is trembling. "Maybe you're just a coward."

Philly Dan whirls around and faces me, eyes blazing, chest heaving, his fists balled up as if ready to fight. "Don't ever say that again, Cato! Ever! I'd give *anything* if I could've stopped this from happening."

His hot breath is inches from my face. I know I shouldn't have said what I said, but I'm mad as a hornet. I look right at him. "If anything bad happens to Isaac, it'll be your fault."

Philly Dan's eyes are on fire now. Towering over me, he leans down, grabs me under both arms, lifts me high in the air, and shakes me so hard it feels like things are rattling around inside. I grab hold of his shoulders, terrified.

Then, as quick as it started, Philly Dan's anger dies, and he lowers me to the ground.

"Sorry, li'l brother." He takes off his Monarchs cap, then puts it back on. He bends forward, almost touching the ground, then stands straight up again. "Isaac's going to be all right. No bones are broken. He's not hurt as bad as it seemed with all that blood."

"Okay," I say, slowly.

We walk in silence again, until I say, "Tell me something about where you left the satchels so I can figure out where it is."

"Crepe myrtle bushes. *Big* ones."

"That could be only one place."

It's not long before we're at the county line between Pender and New Hanover. Years ago, somebody planted crepe myrtle bushes to mark the boundary. There's more here than anywhere else, and they're huge.

Philly Dan turns around in a circle, pulls off his cap, and scratches his head. "Man! Which one did I hide them under?"

I look around too…but a chill comes over me. I try not to imagine what happened here. Was Isaac scared? Did he think he was gonna die? And then the sick feeling in the pit of my stomach comes back.

Maybe this is what happened to Daddy Mo. Only worse.

"Here!" yells Philly Dan from behind a tall bush.

He pulls out two satchels and sets them upright. One is brown with gold-colored latches. He lays it on the ground, opens it, and runs his fingers through the things inside. "I didn't have much, but it's all here. See if it looks like Isaac's stuff is all right."

When I lay the black satchel on the ground and open it, memories spill out.

Gran and Papa Vee gave this satchel to Isaac two years ago, the morning he left for Kansas City. It was Saturday. Rev came by to eat with us. We had a big breakfast of grits and eggs, and we sat around the table talking and laughing until ten in the morning. Then Isaac and Papa Vee and Rev got into the pickup truck and headed off to Wilson's Store, where the buses stop if you're going out of town.

I was so jealous. I remember how much I wanted to go with Isaac.

Everything in his satchel is neatly folded. I shift the layers of socks, underwear, shirts, and pants just to see what's there. Oh my lordy! At the very bottom is Daddy Mo's baseball glove, the one he used the last season he played with the Kansas City Monarchs!

The last season he was alive.

It's old, and the leather is cracked, but the feel of it is magical. In my mind, I see Daddy Mo standing on the mound in Kansas City, the glove on his left hand, throwing fastballs and curveballs at any batter unlucky enough to face him. Then I see myself standing there someday. Being in this family, that's the place I'm bound to be.

I smile, then stuff the glove back to the bottom and close the satchel. For just a moment, it seems like Daddy Mo is right here. A feeling of warmth and fullness comes over me, and I know Daddy Mo's spirit will always be with me.

Me and Philly Dan head home along the road, swinging the satchels back and forth. My thoughts are jumbled, but mostly I'm praying that Isaac will be able to play baseball like he did before.

"You hear something?" I turn my head sideways to catch the sound better.

"Not a thing," says Philly Dan.

But it's there, a low rumble in the distance, getting closer and closer—and then I see a green pickup truck coming toward us. It's driving fast, a cloud of dust behind it, and suddenly it's right on top of us.

*"Jump!"* I dive into Philly Dan's chest and fling us off the road. Just as we hit the ground, the pickup truck roars past. We lay still, our faces in the dirt, until it's quiet again.

"Blazes!" gasps Philly Dan. "What was that?"

I shrug and shake my head. We get up off the ground, but before we take even one step, I say, "Wait."

"What now?"

"I don't know. A feeling." There were plenty of times when Gran had a "feeling," and she was never wrong. I cock my head to one side again and listen. The pickup truck is coming back.

I tug at Philly Dan's arm and we crash into the bushes.

"There it is!" I point. The truck is going much slower now, and someone's leaning out of the window, their white hands holding something long and black.

"Oh lordy! Duck!" I yell, pulling Philly Dan down with me for the second time.

*Kapow! Kapow! Kapow!*

Shots fly over our heads and land somewhere behind us. I hold my breath and lie very still. If the shooters get out of the truck and come looking for us, we're goners. But the sound of the engine fades as the truck drives away.

I let out a long breath. *What if they come back?*

"We better get goin'," I say, turning my head to listen again. Then I look at Philly Dan. He's lying face down in the dirt, not moving at all.

"You can get up now."

I touch Philly Dan lightly on the back, but he still doesn't move.

"Philly Dan?" I say, softly at first, then louder. "Philly Dan!"

# Chapter 14
## UNWELCOMED GUEST

Can't figure why Philly Dan is still lying on the ground. There's no blood anywhere and I don't think he got shot. Country boys learn to shoot at an early age, so if they had meant to hit us, they would have. But why were those white boys shooting at us anyway?

I place one hand on Philly Dan's back to see if he's breathing. He is. Thank the Lord. He finally rolls over on his back and looks from side to side. "Are they gone?"

"Don't play games, man! Not today."

"Sorry, li'l brother. It's hard to know what you're supposed to do when there's white boys shooting at you."

For a moment, the two of us just sit there, looking at one another.

"So, this is the South, huh?" says Philly Dan.

*Reckon so* is what I'm thinking, but I don't answer him right away. I think about Daddy Mo...the kitten dangling from a tree...Harlee Junior and the Burgaw boys getting beat up...Isaac lying bloody on the kitchen table...and now, us getting shot at on a country road.

I shrug. "It's home. And we should get goin'."

Me and Philly Dan start walking again, but neither one of us says a word, and we stay close to the trees. When we reach the house, we see folks have gathered to hold vigil for Isaac's recovery. Rev and the deacons from Saint John's Church are still here, along with our neighbors from Spivey's Corner, and even Mr. Harlee Jamison and folks from his church in Burgaw.

All a sudden my mouth goes dry and a wave of fear runs through me. I stop walking and put the satchel down.

"Philly Dan? What if—?"

"Isaac's going to be fine, Cato. I know your grandma Hope and the rest of the ladies patched him up good."

When we cross the front yard to the door, I wave to Papa Vee and the rest of the folks, go inside, and head straight for Isaac's room. Philly Dan follows. Nobody asks us anything.

Isaac isn't in his room. Instead he's lying in Gran and Papa Vee's bed, his head propped up on three pillows and his arms crossed over his chest. He looks peaceful, like he's no longer in pain.

Gran is sitting in a chair beside him, asleep, her Bible in her lap. But she wakes as soon as we step into the room. "You boys were gone a long time."

"We went to fetch Isaac's satchel," I say, holding his black bag out in front of me.

"My, my...A lot's happened since I last saw that," she says.

"Ma'am, did he wake up yet?" asks Philly Dan.

"No, son, but he's sleeping just fine. The good Lord takes over now."

"Yes ma'am." Philly Dan nods, then goes back outside.

I walk up to the bed, lean over, and put my face close to Isaac's. His breath is shallow, but steady.

"Bet you would've been surprised if Isaac had opened his eyes and butted you in the head, like he used to when you were boys," says Gran, a faint smile on her lips.

"Would be a *nice* surprise," I say.

Can't say how it happened, but next thing I know I'm on the floor, kneeling in front of Gran, my head in her lap, crying like I'm five years old.

Gran puts her arms around me, rubbing circles on my back. After a while, I pull myself into the chair next to her and lay my head on her shoulder. We sit there for a long time, Gran humming one of her favorite spirituals and patting her foot, me watching Isaac's chest rise and fall.

I sit straight up when Rev sticks his head just inside the bedroom door. "Mama J? We've got comp'ny."

"We've had company all day, Amos."

"Thought you might want a word with Mr. Luke Blackburnsays Rev, disappearing down the hall."

"Land's sake. Luke don't need no special howdy—but then if Amos was the first one he saw when he got here, I'd better go out and greet him. No telling what my son said to him!"

Gran gets up from her chair, leans over to pull the covers up around Isaac's neck, and kisses his forehead. I follow her out of the bedroom and onto the front porch.

Mr. Luke's gray pickup truck is making its way slowly over the bumpy dirt road that leads to the house. All of the colored folks gathered on the porch and in the yard are watching him. When Mr. Luke's truck rolls into the yard and stops, no one utters a sound. Trace is driving, but he slumps way down so we can only see his eyes and the top of his head. Mr. Luke opens the door, rests his foot on the running board for a moment, and looks around at the crowd.

"Evening, everybody. Mr. Jamison, Mr. Johnson, Miss Mary Agnes." He nods at first one, then another, and another.

"Evening, Mr. Blackburn," everyone says all together.

Mr. Luke walks toward the front porch where Gran and Papa Vee are sitting in the swing. Hope is standing right beside them. Rev is propped on the banister with one leg resting on the porch. Me and Philly Dan are leaning on the banister on the opposite side of the porch. Mr. Luke starts walking up the steps, but stops on the very top one.

"Evening, Vernon. Miss Nina. Children." He nods again at each one and taps the brim of his Sunday hat.

"Evening, Luke," Gran and Papa Vee say.

"Evening, Amos. Good to see you, though I wish it was for different reasons."

"Me too, Luke," Rev says.

"Vernon, Miss Nina, I heard about your boy and I want you to know how sorry I am. Can't figure who would do such a thing. Must have been somebody passing through."

"Weren't nobody passing through, Luke." Rev gets up from the banister and takes a step toward him. "Whoever hurt Isaac was from around here. We've already had some trouble: white boys fightingcolored boys in Burgaw."

Mr. Luke nods and looks at Gran and Papa Vee.

Rev keeps talking. "In fact, we've been having a *lot* of trouble, here lately. Younger white and colored boys fighting one another, white boys meaning to desecrate the church...maybe it's all on account of that baseball game the boys are going to play. Didn't think so at first, but now I'm wondering."

Mr. Luke is looking down and fingering the change in his pockets, jingling the coins.

Rev takes another step toward him. Mr. Luke steps backward onto a lower step. "The Burgaw boys were just scratched up in the fight they had. But Isaac is hurt bad. And it could've been worse."

"Amos, please." Gran gets up from the swing.

"No, no, Miss Nina. Amos is right," says Mr. Luke. "It could have been worse, and I'm glad that it wasn't. I'll pay a visit to Sheriff Pridgeon and see if we can find out who these boys are."

"That's great, Luke. *Now* you want to be the good citizen—a savior, even! Where were you when Moses needed you?" Rev spits out these words. They splatter in the air.

Everybody gasps.

Mr. Luke walks back up the steps and onto the porch. "That's enough, Amos. I would give anything to change what happened. I tried, but I could never find out who attacked Moses. I've been tied up in knots about it for years. May Heaven forgive me, because I wasn't there for him...but I am here now."

"We'll see, Luke. We'll see," says Rev, turning away.

"That's enough, Amos," says Papa Vee, stepping between Rev and Mr. Luke. "This won't bring Moses back. Now, Luke, if you can find out who's fighting our boys and put a stop to it, I'll be grateful."

"I can do that, Vernon, and I will." Mr. Luke tips his hat to Papa Vee and then to Gran. "Good day, all."

He turns and walks down the porch steps. When he gets to the pickup truck, Trace already has the engine running. As soon as Mr. Luke closes the door, Trace guns it and speeds off. The crowd is hushed until the gray pickup disappears.

"Amos Whitfield! You know I didn't raise you to act like that!" cries Gran. "You're a fine preacher, son, but you're blind when it comes to Luke. He can't change the past, and it's time for you to think about forgiveness."

"Don't fuss at me, Mama J. I can't help how I feel." Rev shakes his head.

"If you don't watch out, the grudge you're holding is going to keep you from entering the pearly gates," warns Papa Vee.

"I know." Rev lets out a long breath. "Well, that's enough of that. Where's the apple pie, Mama J?"

"You know where the kitchen is."

Rev goes inside, and I follow him. "Can't let you eat more pie than me," I whisper.

We both get a huge slice of apple pie and sit at the table across from one another. We raise our forks to eat, then hold them in midair for a moment.

The last time we were in the kitchen, Isaac was stretched out on this very table.

"No racing today, Cato. Let's just eat in peace." Rev's eyes look sad.

We finish eating without another word. Somehow the pie doesn't taste as good as usual.

"How 'bout some more?" I say, rising and putting another slice on Rev's plate before he can say anything. I cut a second piece for myself, too. "Rev...*did* Mr. Luke have something to do with Daddy Mo's death?"

He stops chewing.

"Rev?"

"Hasn't Papa Vee talked to you about this?" He clears his throat and looks up at me. "How Mo died and all?"

"No. I've asked him, but he won't tell me very much."

"Did he say why he wouldn't tell you?"

"He said he wanted me and Hope to be children a little longer."

"Oh."

When Rev doesn't say anything else, I straighten up and add, "I'm going on thirteen. Old enough to know how my daddy died and what Mr. Luke's got to do with it."

"You just think you're old enough, Cato."

"So you're not going to tell me either?"

"It's not my place."

"Well, should I hate Mr. Luke? Did he do something wrong enough for me to hate him?"

"No—no. You shouldn't hate anybody."

"But *you* hate him."

"I don't hate him. I just hate what happened to my brother, that's all. I know it's not right to take it out on Luke, but..."

I stare at Rev, waiting.

"Bless the Lord! I sure am full." He gets up from the table and puts his plate on the sideboard. "I'd better walk off some of this pie 'fore I get heartburn."

I stare at my plate as he hurries out of the kitchen.

# Chapter 15

## FORFEIT

Now that most of the people are gone home, the family is holding its own vigil, taking turns sitting by Isaac's bed. We didn't talk about it. It just happened.

I got up three times last night and peeped into Isaac's room. The first time, Gran was there, sitting by the bed, reading her Bible. The second time, Papa Vee was in the chair, and the third time, it was Philly Dan.

It's 'bout daylight, so I figure it's my turn. I put on a shirt, pants, and shoes and go to Isaac's room. Hope is sitting in the chair, a book in her hand, fast asleep. I sneak up beside her and put my mouth close to her ear.

"Wake up, sleeping beauty," I whisper.

"Oh!" Hope drops her book. "Stop it, Cato! You want to wake up Isaac?"

"I'm just playing with you." I stare at Isaac, wishing he *would* wake up—wishing he would talk to us, so we know he's all right.

"I hate that he's hurt...but it will be nice to have him home for a while," says Hope. "When he comes to visit for the week, seems like soon as I get happy, it's time for him to go."

Hope touches Isaac's hand. He stirs for a moment, then lies still again.

"Yeah. I can't wait to hear more stories about the Monarchs barnstorming in the North, playing in D.C. and Philly."

"Barnstorming? Do you and Isaac ever talk about *anything* besides baseball?"

"Sometimes. But what else is there to talk about, really?"

"Well, he told *me* that he saw the Liberty Bell."

"Gee. What do you know."

"And when the Monarchs went to Joplin, Missouri, he saw where Mr. Langston Hughes was born. That's Miss Holmes's favorite colored poet."

"Everybody knows she loves Langston Hughes. She gave me one of his poems to recite next month."

Hope laughs. "I got one to learn too."

"Okay, well. It's my turn now, Hope. You need to move and let me sit a spell."

Hope nods, picks her book up off the floor, and walks out. I settle in the chair, wishing I'd brought the poem I have to learn, but I soon fall asleep myself. Every now and again, I wake, lean over, check on Isaac, and go back to sleep.

'Fore I know anything, Papa Vee is tapping me on the shoulder. "Hey!" I yell, louder than I mean to.

"*Shhh.* Time for us to get on with our day. Your grandma will see after Isaac. You should go to baseball practice after school today—it'll do you good. If Isaac wakes up, we'll call you home."

"Yes suh."

———

At school, everybody knows about what happened, and Miss Holmes draws our lessons from that. We talk about the South and slavery again; about Reconstruction and Jim Crow laws. About how we have to live in colored towns, how we have to work in colored jobs, and how we don't get decent pay for the work we do. I've heard Rev say that he's glad he got the calling to be a preacher, 'cause it's hard for a colored man to make a living any other way.

Whenever she wants to teach us about life, Miss Holmes reads to us from one of her own books. Most times it's a short story or a poem. Today she reads us two poems from *The Weary Blues* by Mr. Langston Hughes. The first, "Mother to Son," is about a colored woman talking to her son about how hard her life has been and how she's not giving up. The next poem, "Dream Variation," is full of hope. Kinda makes being colored feel just right.

When school's out, I thank the Lord. I meet the Rangers out front, and we cross the schoolyard to Walker Field. Papa Vee was right: throwing some baseballs, running, and hitting is just what the Rangers need to lift our spirits.

After an hour or so, Miss Holmes and the other children have all gone home, and Rangers are free to make as much noise as we want. Yelling and talking trash feels so good! We're all having so much fun that no one notices when a red truck turns off of the road in front of the schoolhouse and heads our way. It runs over Miss Holmes's flower bed, rolls right under the sycamore tree, and stops. Two white boys get out.

I know them. Freight Train and Mouse. And they're both wearing red T-shirts. Were they...?

"Is this your ball field?" asks Freight Train, looking around. "Pitiful. No wonder you was trespassing on ours." He grins, showing the gap in front where one of his teeth is missing—prob'ly knocked out in a fight. He pokes Mouse with his elbow, and Mouse nods his head slowly.

"Now you're the one trespassing," I say coldly. "No one invited you here."

Looking at Freight Train makes me sick: me and Mason are still taking care of Moses, but that kitty's still got cigarette scars—don't know if we'll ever give it back to Hope.

"Well if that ain't the pot calling the kettle...what, Mouse?"

"Black!" says Mouse. They laugh.

The Rangers pull in tight behind me, glaring. Freight Train's eyes dart around, like he's counting how many of us there are.

"What do you want, anyway?" I ask.

"Well, I came to do you boys a favor." Freight Train looks sideways at Mouse and smiles. "Heard you had some trouble. One of your players got hurt bad or something. Being shorthanded, you might want to forfeit the game instead of losing outright. Marlins were gonna beat the livin' tar out of you anyways."

*One of our players?* Do they think Isaac is on the team?

Rangers pull in even tighter around me, staring down the white boys.

"You must be dreaming. Rangers will never forfeit. If we play you, we're gonna beat you," I tell him.

"*Yeah!*" the Rangers yell, raising fists in the air.

"That so?" Freight Train rubs his chin. "'Less you forfeit, there might not be enough of you left for a team."

His words hit me like a slap in the face.

Even though I remember the last time we tangled, I'm ready to do it again—but before I can, Raymond D. steps up beside me. "What're you sayin', white boy? Did you and your cousin have anything to do with what happened to Isaac Jones?"

The Rangers mumble and move in even closer, forming a semicircle almost surrounding Freight Train and Mouse.

The two of them pass an uneasy look between them. Beads of sweat form on Mouse's upper lip, and he wipes them off with his shirtsleeve. Freight Train shoves his hands in his pockets and slowly backs away from us. "Y'all need to think hard on what I said. Forfeit the game and save us all a lot of trouble."

Then he whirls around real fast and heads for his truck, Mouse close behind him.

Raymond D. and I start after them, but Mason grabs our arms and pulls us back. "No! We'll whup them on the ball field. That's what Rev said we ought to do."

Freight Train guns the engine of his pickup truck and steps on the gas, driving backward across the schoolyard. On the road, he passes Mr. Luke Blackburn's old gray pickup truck coming toward us. It stops under the sycamore tree. Trace gets out.

"Hey, was that Freight Train? What in the world was he doing here?"

"He wanted the Rangers to forfeit the ball game. Said we might lose players between now and game time if we don't," I say.

"What?" says Trace, going pale. "He said *that*?"

"He did. And what do you have to say about it?" demands Raymond D.

"Yeah, what?" says Skeeter.

Trace looks around and sees how the Rangers are clumped together, how they're frowning. He seems to be measuring his words now. "Look fellas, I say we play the ball game when Isaac gets well. He can come and watch."

"You mean…you don't want us to forfeit the game?" asks CP.

"No," says Trace. "Marlins want to play this game so we can beat you."

The Rangers start to mumbling louder now:

"Uh-uh."

"No way."

"Dream on."

"How is Isaac?" asks Trace. "Is he up and about yet?"

Before I can answer, I hear my name called.

*"Cato! Come quick!"*

Hope is running across the schoolyard, arms pumping, skirt flying, her bare feet kicking up dust. "It's Isaac! He woke up! He woke up!"

As soon as Hope knows I've heard her, she turns back toward home. And in no time I catch up to her.

As we run, I whisper a prayer of thanks under my breath. My heart beats like it will jump out of my chest. I'm so excited.

And so scared.

Behind me, footsteps pound the road like a herd of buffalo. The Pender County Rangers are running with us too.

# Chapter 16
## ISAAC

When we get to the house, I take the porch steps two at a time and nearly pull the hinges off the screen door as I rush inside. Hope is right behind me. The Rangers wait for us outside.

Isaac is sitting up in bed, three pillows behind him, eating a plate of grits and eggs. Gran is in the chair next to him, and Papa Vee and Philly Dan are standing at the foot of the bed.

Isaac's face lights up when me and Hope walk in. It's been a day since the attack, and Isaac doesn't look like himself. Can't wait 'til he does.

"'Bout time you showed up." He flashes a feeble smile.

Hope walks over to the bed and kisses his forehead.

"Hey, beautiful," he whispers. She beams.

I'm standing near the door, biting down hard on the inside of my mouth to keep back the tears.

"You all right, son?" asks Papa Vee, gazing at me.

"Yes suh."

"You ain't too old for hugging, are you?" Isaac asks me.

I shake my head as I walk over to the bed. Then I bend down and hug him, being careful not to squeeze too hard. As I pull away, Isaac puts a finger in his plate, scoops up some warm grits, and smears it on my nose. We all bust out laughing.

"Praise the Lord," says Gran, smiling so wide her dimples show. "It's been a while since we've all laughed like this."

"What are the Rangers up to this spring?" asks Isaac.

I tell him about us having a match with the Marlins. I describe Poplar Field, too: how Mr. Luke built it brand-new for the Marlins, with real bases 'stead of flat rocks set in the ground, and with a pitcher's mound that looks like the ones in the postcards he sends me of stadiums in Chicago and D.C.

"Can't wait to see that," says Isaac.

"Yeah," I say, looking at the floor, knowing I've left a lot out.

"Enough talking, now," Gran says. "Isaac needs to rest."

"Yes ma'am," says Papa Vee. We all follow him out of the room.

Me and Philly Dan go outside, where the Rangers are waiting in some shade. When we tell them that Isaac is talking and laughing and eating grits, they raise a cheer.

"We can rest easy now," says Raymond D, grinning.

I nod, but easy's not how I feel.

We talk about Isaac and baseball for a bit, and then the Rangers scatter for home.

———

I'm glad that our house feels happy again, at least. Isaac is talking and laughing and teasing me like he used to. Gran sings *Swing Low, Sweet Chariot* while she makes supper. Hope smiles every time you look at her, and Papa Vee sits on the porch steps whittling and humming.

When it's time to eat, Isaac is sleeping, and I'm disappointed he can't be at the table with us. As soon as we're done, me and Hope get up and rush to the back of the house, bumping into one another at the door of his sickroom.

"Gran said to let him sleep!" scolds Hope.

"Then go away and let him sleep."

"That means *you. I'll peep in just to check on him.*"

"All right." I roll my eyes.

But I still want to be near Isaac, so I go outside and sit below the open window of his room to finish my homework. I still have to memorize that poem from Mr. Langston Hughes's book, *The Weary Blues*. It's called

"Epilogue"—Miss Holmes says that's not really a title, just a word that tells you it's the end of the book, but he used it as one anyway.

I like this poem so much that the words come back to me easily as I whisper it to myself. It's full of hope. I'm glad it's not about some kind of sorrow that colored folks have to go through. Things like that weigh heavy on my heart sometimes.

After a while, I stand up and peek through the window. The room is silent and Isaac lies peaceful and still. Then I see Philly Dan come in, so I crouch down under the window again before raising my head just enough to look inside. Philly Dan's back is to me.

"You awake, buddy?" Philly Dan kneels beside Isaac's bed.

"Yeah."

"Hey man, I'm sorry. Sorry. Sorry. Sorry. Can't say it enough times."

"Not your fault." Isaac speaks softly.

"If I'd been on time, if I hadn't missed the bus, none of this would've happened."

"Can't say that. There was a bunch of them."

"It kills me to see you all busted up like this."

"Not your fault," Isaac says again.

"Do you forgive me?" asks Philly Dan.

"No need. We're brothers."

"Brothers or no, I plan to spend the rest of my life making this up to you. I'll start with Cato—gonna give him and the Rangers some lessons on how to win their ball game. That's what you would do if you could."

"Yeah," agrees Isaac. "I would."

"I'll teach Cato some of Satchel's pitching tricks and give him some pointers on how to hit like Josh."

"*I* want those lessons," says Isaac.

Philly Dan lets out a hearty laugh. Can't see Isaac, but he must be smiling.

"I'm just glad you're all right, man."

"Tears? Come on, Philly."

"All right." There's a scrape of chair legs as Philly Dan stands. "I better let you get some rest before Gran comes in here and beats me with a broomstick."

"She just might," teases Isaac.

Philly Dan walks out, and I'm hoping he won't come around to the side of the house and see me. I peek in one more time—then drop down in a hurry when Papa Vee comes in next.

Cautiously, I raise myself up again, spying. Like Philly Dan, he stands by Isaac's bed with his back to the window.

"You're looking so much better, son. Thank God." Papa Vee shoves his hands into the pockets of his overalls. "Who did this, Isaac? Don't talk a lot. I just want to know if you saw anything."

"Happened so fast, Papa Vee. Got off the bus. Something hit me. I fell down. White boys…and something red…are the only things I know for sure."

I feel blood rush through my whole body, feel the tips of my ears burn. Red again. Just like Harlee Junior.

Just like Freight Train and Mouse.

# Chapter 17
## SPRING TRAINING

At last! Now that Isaac is on the mend, the Rangers can finally get back to playing baseball. Today Philly Dan is going to give some lessons that will help us beat those lyin' New Hanover boys.

Now, we don't really know how good the Marlins are. (The one chance we had to find out, we were too busy playing shadow ball.) But whether they're good or not, I'm excited, and I know we'll beat them. Philly Dan may just be a shortstop—and he's not Satchel Paige—but he is a professional baseball player with the Kansas City Monarchs. Have to pinch myself when I think how close my family is to this Negro League team.

I wake up earlier than usual, dress myself in a hurry, and head to the kitchen to find something to eat. Philly Dan walks in after me.

"Do you always eat molasses biscuits for breakfast?" he asks, watching me closely.

"Yep. Ever since I can remember. Me and Daddy Mo used to race to see who could eat the most."

"Uh-huh. I'm starting to like molasses biscuits too." He grabs two biscuits, lays them out on the table, slathers molasses on them, and takes his first bite. "Well, today's the day, Cato. I'm going to teach you some things that will change your game...maybe change your life."

"You can teach me how to be a better pitcher? Even as a shortstop?"

"I can play a lot of positions. I'm kind of like Double Duty Ratcliff of the Memphis Red Sox. Pitching is the thing I love most, but I'm not good enough for that, professionally."

"When did you ever pitch?"

"All through high school! I pitched, played shortstop—was a catcher, too."

"Does Isaac know this?"

"Sure he does. I study Satchel and the rest of them every chance I get. Times when we don't have a game, Isaac lets me practice pitching with him."

"Wow!"

"You ready?" asks Philly Dan, shoving the last of his molasses biscuit into his mouth.

I stuff some extra biscuits in a paper sack, like always, and run toward the door. "Are you coming?" I yell over my shoulder.

Our walk to Walker Field goes fast, and it's no surprise that the Rangers swarm around Philly Dan as soon as we arrive, pushing one another out of the way to get close.

Skeeter jumps in front of everyone else. "Hey, do you know Willie Wells? I say he's one of the best shortstops in Negro League baseball! Can you get him to come to Sycamore Grove?"

"No, let's invite a catcher, like Biz Mackey!" says Mason.

"Josh Gibson! How could we want anybody besides the best home-run hitter in baseball?" Hank yells.

"If anybody's gonna come to Sycamore Grove, it's got to be Satchel Paige, the best pitcher in the whole world," I say firmly.

Philly Dan raises both hands in the air. "Fellas, last I heard, Isaac and me are the only Negro League players planning to be in Sycamore Grove anytime soon. If anything changes, I'll let you know. Now, stop talking and let's play some baseball!"

"All right!" the Rangers yell.

First, Philly Dan makes us run laps around the ball field to warm up. Then everybody practices throwing, hitting, and fielding while me and Philly Dan head for the pitcher's mound.

"How come Cato's getting special time with you?" asks Skeeter, following behind us for a spell.

Philly Dan raises one eyebrow. "He's your pitcher. You want to win or not?"

"We want to win," agrees Skeeter, running to join the rest of the Rangers.

"Throw me some fastballs when I get in the catcher's spot," Philly Dan tells me. "I want to see what you've got."

I wait for him to get in place, then wind up and throw six fastballs. Each pitch is faster, more deliberate than the last. With each one, I use the windup I started just a year ago: I raise my left leg higher and higher off the ground before hurling the ball toward home plate. By the sixth pitch, my leg almost grazes the side of my cheek. By the last pitch, Philly Dan is standing straight up and staring at me, both hands on his hips. He shakes his head very slowly, then walks out to me on the mound.

"Say, li'll'il brother. That's a mighty unusual windup you got there."

"Unusual?"

"That means different."

"You mean...bad?" My stomach turns. I don't want to hear that I'm the worst pitcher he's ever seen.

"No—not bad. I'm just saying it's odd. How long you been raising your leg up so high its kissing your face?"

"'Bout a year."

"Why?"

"Why what?"

"Why do you pitch like that?"

"It works. I can throw the ball much harder and it lands where I want it to. Everything flows."

"It flows?"

"Yeah. I got that word from Rev."

"Your uncle? The preacher?"

"Yep. When I asked him how he can preach such great sermons every Sunday, he said it was easy as water flowing downhill—if you start in the right place."

Philly Dan's eyes light up. The left side of his mouth crinkles in the hint of a smile. "I see. You tell Isaac about this?"

"Not yet."

"Okaaay! We'll surprise him later. Let's get on with our lesson for today."

Philly Dan puts his arm around my shoulder and leans in close. "A pitcher's got to have some tricks up his sleeve, Cato—got to throw a pitch or two that nobody's looking for and can't figure out when they see it. That's what Satchel does. That man's got some crazy pitches that nobody can throw but him—and almost nobody can hit them, either. Like 'the hesitation.' "

"Hes-i-tation? Why they call it that?"

"Well, it's a fastball coming at you, but slower than you think it would. Somewhere between winding up and letting go of the ball, Satchel slows his arm down. Most batters are so busy trying to figure out where the ball is and what the heck it's doing, they don't even swing the bat. And that's a strike for sure."

We both laugh. "Are you gonna teach me how to pitch that?"

"Naw! That one belongs to Satchel Paige."

"So you're saying what I *really* need is a few tricks up my sleeve—a few pitches the Marlins won't be looking for."

"That's the plan, but we'll start off slow. I'll teach you how to throw a slider first."

"Man! When we're done, those white boys won't have a chance."

"Calm down, now." Philly Dan motions with his hands. "Remember, we don't know how good their pitcher is yet."

Philly Dan takes a baseball out of his pocket and holds it out in front of him. "I'll teach you how to throw the slider today." He holds the ball with his fingers on top and his thumb underneath. "Now let me see you try it."

I place my fingers on the baseball just like Philly Dan did.

"Good. Now, throw the slider like your fastball, but not as hard. Throw it nice and easy."

Philly Dan goes to the catcher's spot, and I throw about ten sliders over home plate. My new windup helps me to have better control, so the ball goes right in Philly's glove. When I'm done, he walks back out to the mound.

"Wicked, Cato! That kick of yours really helps you to put some bite into the ball. I'm going to leave here with my arm in a sling if I'm not careful. Let's get Mason over here, and a batter, too—let you practice switching from your fastball to the slider."

"You know, I can pitch a fastball slow, fast, or lightning fast," I say. *Sort of like Satchel Paige and his hesitation*, I think.

"That's even better. Let me see some of that."

Might as well call in our catcher and our best batter. "Mason! Hank!" I yell.

Hank steps into the batter's box and raises his bat, ready for the pitch. I throw four fastballs over home plate and Hank hits them all to center field. Then I place my fingers near the seams of the ball, just so, like Philly Dan showed me, and throw the slider. Hank swings. He misses, then raises his bat for the next pitch. Another slider. Another strike.

"Hey!" yells Hank. "What was that? Weren't your fastball, that's for sure."

"We call it a slider," I say.

Five more times I throw the slider, leaning hard into my unusual windup. And five times, the ball lands in Mason's glove without Hank's bat ever touching it. By now the rest of the Rangers have gathered near home plate to watch.

"Mercy, Cato!" says Smokey Joe. "If you've got a new pitch that Hank can't hit, those lyin' Devils don't have a chance."

Then Smokey Joe runs to the mound, grabs me around the waist, and lifts me off the ground. "Cato's our secret weapon. We're gonna win this game for sure."

The Rangers rush to the mound and join Smokey Joe in holding me up. My teammates carry me around the field for a full lap before they put me down. We slap hands and scatter for home, certain that we'll win the showdown with the Marlins. The speed I get with my new pitching windup is the Rangers secret weapon, but I can't help but wonder what surprises the Marlins have waiting for us.

# Chapter 18
## GAME DAY

It's game day.

Game. Day!

My stomach is full of knots, and my heart is pounding. I had to wash my sweaty underarms twice before I put my clothes on. Man! The Rangers *have* to win this game against the Marlins, but I worry again about how we're playing in the dark—we don't know a thing about how good the Marlins are. We *really* should've been finding out when we were fooling around with shadow ball...but that was just too much fun to pass up.

I'm blaming Mr. Luke for some of this. When he said that the Rangers could practice with the Marlins, he was thinking about him and Daddy Mo. I just know it. Seems like what he wants most of all is for me and that lyin' sweet-potato-headed son of his to be friends. Never!

Isaac sticks his head inside the pantry curtain. Knowing that he feels well enough to go to the game makes my heart leap. "Cato? You coming to breakfast, man? Everybody's waiting for you."

Gran made an extra good breakfast this morning. Rev is hunched over his plate, shoveling in eggs and pancakes and bragging about how happy he'll be when the Rangers whup Mr. Luke's boys. Isaac and Philly Dan give me a long, encouraging look.

They're expecting a lot from me. The whole team is. A lump of doubt forms in my throat.

I sit down to an empty plate that Gran soon fills with piping hot food. I only push it around. My stomach is still doing flip-flops, and eating is the last thing I want to do.

Isaac shoves the last of a pancake into his mouth and pushes back from the table. "Cato. Philly. Game on. Let's go."

"Wait, I need to get my cap," I say, dashing into the pantry.

My Rangers baseball cap is on the bottom shelf next to Daddy Mo's Kansas City Monarchs cap. For a moment, my hand lingers, not sure which one I should wear. I grab Daddy Mo's cap, bury my face in it, and breathe in the smell of it. Then I put it back in place, grab my Rangers cap, pull it down snug on my head, and rush out to join Isaac and Philly Dan. We're headed to Walker Field, where the Rangers will gather first, then on to Poplar Field.

Soon as we get into the front yard, Mason shows up.

"Anybody going to a ball game today?" he yells, running past us toward the road without stopping. I hurry to catch up with him. Isaac and Philly Dan take their time behind us.

"I'm feeling good about this game, Cato. We've got a secret weapon and they don't!"

"We don't know *what* they've got, Mason, but I feel good about having the slider and a fastball to throw."

"Of course, we'll be in deep doo-doo if those boys can hit your pitches."

"They can't hit what they can't see! With my new windup, I can throw every pitch so much faster."

"*Secret weapon!*" Mason says again.

When we get to Walker Field, Rangers slap each other on the back and stand around grinning, talking, and admiring how good we look in our uniforms. They're cream-colored with red stripes, and our caps are the same. At the end of last season, Isaac bought them for us in a secondhand store in Kansas City. Over the winter, Gran and some of the church ladies cut them down to fit us and added a red *R* in the place where a pocket ought to be.

"You boys look like a professional baseball team." Philly Dan grins.

"Man, I feel so good, I could run around a ball field ten times," brags CP.

"Save that energy for the game," warns Philly Dan.

"Now listen, fellas," says Isaac. "This is the very first game between a white and a colored team in New Hanover County. We know that Mr. Luke is excited, but some white folks don't want it to happen. And they might let you know just how much."

"But here's the thing," continues Philly Dan. "You've got to shut out all of the noise and think about *baseball*. Rangers are a winning team, and each and every one of you help to make that happen. So let's show these folks what you're made of. Rangers are here to win!"

"Here to win!" the Rangers yell.

"And," says Philly Dan, "let's play smart, fellas. Don't show them all of your stuff right away. Play it slow and easy for the first three innings or so."

"Right," says Isaac. "Around the fourth or fifth inning, throw everything you've got at them. Got it? Easy in the beginning and wicked in the end. That's the smart way to play."

"All right, Rangers!" yells Philly Dan. "Let's…"

"Play ball!" he and Isaac say together.

We form a huddle, put our right arms in the center, count, "Three, two, one," and yell, "Rangers! Rangers! Let's win!"

Then we head to Poplar Field, running two abreast, slow and easy to save energy and to make sure everybody sees how good we look in our uniforms.

"Where the colored folks?" asks Skeeter. "Where the girls that stand on the side of the road and cheer when we're going to a game?"

I look at the people walking on the road with us. Men and boys in small groups, hands shoved deep in their pockets, talking to one another in low voices. Don't see any women or girls with picnic baskets, all dressed up and ready to have fun. That's what a ball game is like most times. Don't see many colored folks either. Guess they don't feel welcome at the white folks' ball field, even though Mr. Luke said they could come.

"Rangers! Rangers!" Twenty or so boys from Tidewater Colored League teams run past us now. Seeing them brings a smile to my face. Rangers wave as they pass.

"I feel safer now," says Mason.

"Me too."

As soon as these words leave my mouth, a flash of red sends a chill all through me. .

There's a line of red-shirted boys just ahead of us, stretched across the road, walking real slow. If Rangers keep running, we'll crash into them. I wave my hand in the air, slow down, and start walking. Rangers do the same.

The fellas in red T-shirts step off the road and line up on the side of it, clapping their hands as we pass by. My spirits rise for a moment. Are they welcoming us?

Then we hear a whining sound coming from them. It starts low in their throats and gets louder and louder. Soon, they're all barking like dogs.

"What in the world are these boys up to?" asks Mason.

I don't answer, but my eyes dart from one side of the road to the other, wondering if they're going to do something dangerous. Then Isaac and Philly Dan run to the head of the Rangers pack, one on our right side, the other on our left.

"*Rangers! Double time!*" Isaac shouts.

Heads held high, Rangers sprint onto Poplar Field, leaving the boys in red far behind.

# Chapter 19

## REBEL YELL

The crowd at Poplar Field is mighty sparse.

Some folks prob'ly stayed home 'cause they don't want to watch a matchup between a white and a colored team. I can spot a few friends of Mr. Luke, at least: they kind of look like him and they dress like him in overalls, plaid shirts, and Marlins baseball caps. Still no women or girls in sight. They were expecting trouble, I reckonr. Rev, Papa Vee, Mr. Harlee Jamison, and Harlee Junior stand up and wave their arms in the air wildly to make sure we see them. The builder, Mr. D. K. Johnson, and boys from the Tidewater Colored League teams are sitting right next to them.

I smile and wave as the Rangers circle the field once for good measure. That's when the boys in red appear at the edge of the ball field, hooting loudly.

*What in the world?*

Me and Mason look at one another and shake our heads. The red-shirted boys move to sit on the row of bleachers closest to third base, forcing some children out of their seats.

On a signal from Mr. Luke, the teams gather in the middle of the ball field facing one another. The Pender County Rangers are in our new cream-colored uniforms with red stripes and the New Hanover Marlins are in navy blue-and-white-striped uniforms with an *M* on the front where a pocket ought to be. Copycats!

The umpire, a friend of Mr. Luke's I reckon, stands in the middle of the circle, holding a buffalo nickel. "Okay, boys. Pick your poison," he says. "The winner can choose to be visitors or the home team."

"Heads," I say, real fast so no one else can claim it.

Trace looks at me sideways. "Tails," he says.

The umpire tosses the nickel high into the air. It flips. And falls. The call is tails.

"Home team," says Trace.

I shrug. That means Rangers are first at bat.

Man! What happens next is not something Rangers are used to: right away, Trace Blackburn shows us what a good pitcher he is.

Our best batters, Hank, Smokey Joe, and Raymond D. are at the top of the Rangers lineup. Hank raises his bat into position. The look on his face says he thinks he can hit anything. But Trace winds up and throws a pitch so hard and so fast that Hank doesn't even swing at it.

"Strike," yells the umpire.

Hank's forehead wrinkles. He lowers his bat, leans it against his leg, and rubs his eyes with both hands. Then he raises his bat into position again.

"Strike!" we hear the umpire say, with Hank still standing there holding his bat high.

Me and Mason look at one another. "Uh-oh," we say.

Hank raises his bat again and the umpire yells, "Strike!"

Oh lordy. It's the bottom of the first inning and our very best batter struck out looking!

Smokey Joe and Raymond D. step into the batter's box, one right after the other. They raise their bats. I see them do this, but all I can remember is the umpire yelling, "Strike!" six times. Side out! Our turn at bat is shorter than we would ever have imagined.

There's more bad news for the Rangers. Our secret weapon is a dud. I strike out a few batters, but Marlins get two runs off of me in each one of the first four innings. The rest of the team can't stop them. When it's our turn at bat, Rangers also seem to be playing the same inning over and over. In the first four innings, every one of our batters strikes out. At the top of the fifth inning, Hank hits a home run, getting us on the scoreboard, at least!

| | 1st | 2nd | 3rd | 4th | 5th | 6th | 7th | 8th | 9th | Runs | Hits | Errors |
|---|---|---|---|---|---|---|---|---|---|---|---|---|
| Rangers | 0 | 0 | 0 | 0 | 1 | | | | | 1 | 1 | 0 |
| Marlins | 2 | 2 | 2 | 2 | | | | | | 8 | 12 | 2 |

It's now the bottom of the fifth inning and Marlins turn at bat. Rangers are down by seven runs. I step onto the mound, feeling like the world is on my shoulders. I know I can count on good fielding from my teammates, but it's my job to strike out as many batters as I can. Didn't do that in the first four innings. Don't know why. Couldn't get the feel of my new windup, I reckon. And my sliders didn't land the way I wanted them to.

But I have to be a lot better now.

I take in a deep breath, raise my glove up to my face, the baseball cradled in my right hand, and stare at the batter. He's the first fella that I faced when the game started. I struck him out then. I can strike him out now. Three fastballs and I do. We have the first out.

Freight Train is up next. He's gotten two hits off me and scored a run in the third inning. I want to strike him out so bad I can taste it. I raise my glove to my face, aiming to rattle Freight Train by staring at him long and hard. Must've forgotten who he is. Now he's staring back at me, his mouth turned down in a frown.

I close my eyes for a moment, trying to call up all the inspiration that I can from Daddy Mo, Papa Vee, Isaac, Rev, Philly Dan, and every other colored man I admire. That's what I'll need if my new windup is going to help my pitching the way I want it to. I take in a deep breath, raise my left leg high in the air, lean back slightly, then lunge forward, letting the baseball fly out of my hand. It lands with a *thunk* in Mason's glove, just where I want it.

"Strike!" the umpire calls.

Freight Train's forehead wrinkles. His eyes widen. He lowers his bat and turns to look at Mason. When he faces me again, I see fire in Freight

Train's eyes. He raises his bat again. I take in a deep breath. Gonna put him away for sure. I lift my leg even higher than before and release the baseball as hard as I can. Again, I hear a satisfying *thunk* as the ball lands in Mason's glove.

"Strike!" the umpire yells.

Two strikes. Freight Train's face is racked with anger. This time, 'stead of looking at Mason, he nods at the boys in red. Then he plants his feet in position again, gripping his bat even tighter. I smile inside, careful not to let Freight Train see satisfaction on my face. I wind up again, this time, raising my left leg almost up to my cheekbone, and throw another fastball right into Mason's glove.

"Strike three!" the umpire yells.

No one is surprised when Freight Train throws his bat to the ground and stalks off the field. The boys in red bang the bricks they brought with them against the bleachers, showing that they don't like what just happened.

I get a queasy feeling in my stomach. What are these fellas gonna do next if they don't like something? Trace Blackburn comes to bat now. Leaning hard on my new pitching windup, he's almost as easy to strike out as Freight Train was, though he does manage to foul off the tip of his bat a couple of times. As he walks off the field, Trace turns to look back at me. What I see in his face is surprise. And...

Admiration.

"Side out!" the umpire calls.

"*Hallelujah!*" I yell.

The Rangers and all of our fans cheer at the top of our lungs. We're down by seven runs, but proud that the Marlins didn't score in the fifth inning. Maybe our luck will change and we'll win the game. Our happiness is soon crushed. Marlins fans fill the air with loud booing. The boys in red have left their seats and gathered at the edge of the field. They cup both hands around their mouths and bark like dogs. Then Digger throws his head way back and lets out a loud and mournful howl. It starts low and rises to a pitch that is so high, it hurts my ears.

A rebel yell!

I've heard a sound like this once before. I was ten years old. Me and Papa Vee had gone hunting for rabbits in some woods on the edge of New Hanover County; someone we never saw did it to scare us off. Felt like the hair on my head stood straight up. My heart was pounding!

Papa Vee said that during the Civil War, Confederate armies made the yell when they were going into battle. Hearing it now—at the first game between a white and a colored baseball team in the county—chills me to the bone. These boys remind me of things about the South that I don't like to think about. Two words come to mind:

*Rebel.*

*Clan.*

Southern boys in a tight group.

The sound of more barking gets my attention now. This time the dogs are real! Four boys from the Rebel Clan are moving onto the ball field, each one guiding a large dog that's slobbering at the mouth and straining against its leash. Someone must have brought them here on the back of a pickup truck! Won't take these dogs long to reach us if the boys let them go!

Next thing I know, somebody grabs my arms, one on each side, lifting me off the ground. They're running with me now.

"Rev's truck," is all Philly Dan says.

He and Raymond D. let go of my arms. My feet touch the dirt and we're racing. I turn my head and some of the Rangers are climbing on the back of Papa Vee's truck with Isaac at the wheel.

Rev starts moving as soon as we jump on the back of his truck. We speed away from Poplar Field, raising a cloud of dust.

I half expect the Rebel Clan and their dogs to be chasing us, but when I look back, there's nobody there. After a mile or so, we turn off onto a side road and head into the woods. My Rangers crew—the ones with me—sits in the back of Rev's truck, shoulder to shoulder, our knees drawn up to our chests. The truck bounces up and down on the uneven dirt road. Every now and again it hits a big bump, and we all wince. I wonder if the other half of the team is having a rough ride too.

I close my eyes and see all of us on the ball field again, out of our minds with happiness when Hank hits a home run...What a sweet moment that was. Cheering loudly when the Marlins batters strike out. The sour look on Freight Train's face and the anger in his eyes were satisfying.

But the Rangers paid a price for all that joy. And as we speed away from Poplar Field, I wonder how high the cost will really be.

# Chapter 20
## SANCTUARY

Papa Vee, Rev, and Mr. Luke waited until last night to tell us about the plan- the one that we'd need if the Rangers won the game. No one thought, though, that we'd have to get away before the game even ended.

To confuse anybody who might be following us, we split into two groups. Ours is headed to Saint John's Church, the other to Mr. Harlee Jamison's church in Burgaw.

"How long are we gonna hide out here, Rev?" I ask, gathered with the Rangers at the back of the church.

"Can't say. I'll leave in a minute, go check with our scouts, see if there's trouble brewing and how much."

I frown. Rev's gonna ask us to act like cowards again. "What're we supposed to do while you're gone?"

Rev looks at me the way Gran does when I've got on her last nerve. "You boys are smart enough to keep quiet 'til I get back. Don't raise a racket. Nobody knows you're here, and it's best to keep it that way."

Rev ducks out to his truck. When he comes back, he's got a shotgun in each hand. Rangers look at one another, our eyebrows raised.

"Is there something you didn't tell us?" asks Mason.

He looks uneasy, like he did when the two of us were in Mr. Luke's store. But I'm excited. Maybe we won't have to be cowards after all.

"Well, boys, Sheriff Pridgeon is supposed to keep an eye out for trouble, but—"

"He might not," I say, knowing that the sheriff doesn't always look out for colored folk.

"Now, if anybody comes looking for you, just know they'll meet an army when they get here," says Rev.

The Rangers look at one another again.

"Um, Rev? We ain't no army," says Skeeter.

"No, but there's an army of neighbors and church folks ready to stand with you!"

"Where are they?" asks Raymond D.

"Well, son, a convoy would've shined a light on where we were going. They'll be coming soon, one or two trucks at a time."

"Then why're you leaving these shotguns with us, Rev?" I ask.

Rev lays them on the pews closest to the doors. "Well...I don't want you to get caught with your skivvies down."

"Which one of us are you 'specting to use those guns?" asks Skeeter, looking around at everyone.

"I hope *nobody* needs to use them, but if you do, remember that baseball teams follow the same rules on and off the field. The captain makes the decisions."

All eyes fall on me.

"Don't touch these guns unless you figure that you have no other choice," Rev tells me sternly.

"Yes suh," I say quietly.

Rev crosses his arms. "I want you to hunker down and wait. Sit on the floor, so you're lower than the windows in case somebody rides by." He walks toward the door, his voice fading. "Most likely, nothing at all will happen."

A hush falls over us after he leaves.

We've spent a lifetime of Sunday mornings in here, feeling safe and loved. The church feels very different now, but it's still hard to believe we might be in danger. Tired from the game and the excitement, we hunker down and sleep for a while.

When my eyes snap open, late-afternoon sun is streaming through the windows.

Me and my crew are sitting shoulder to shoulder, our legs stretched out in front of us, our heads low. The same windows that bring in sunlight during Sunday services now threaten to give our dark bodies away. I wonder how Smokey Joe and the rest of the fellas are doing in Burgaw.

I take in a deep breath and blow it out slowly. I'm bored with sitting around like this, and sort of mad 'cause we're hiding.

I twist, then stretch my arms wide, bumping Mason and Hank in the face on purpose.

"Hey!" they both cry, coming awake.

"Shhh! Rev said to be quiet," I whisper, almost laughing.

Now everyone's awake. For a moment, we just look at one another and shake our heads, like we can't figure out what we're doing here.

"My backside is hurting," whines Skeeter. "I need to stand up."

Before anybody can stop him, he rises right in front of the window, stretches, and yawns. Then he drops back down to the floor in a hurry.

We all sit straight up.

"What is it?" I ask.

"Truck's coming!" Skeeter shakes his head. "Just one. And it's not Rev...!"

# Chapter 21
## TRAPPED

I stand up slowly and peep out of the small window in the door of the church.

"What do you see, Cato?" whispers CP.

I wave my hand for him to be quiet. "Stay down, fellas," I order.

A pickup truck, so old and rusted out I can't tell what color it is, rolls into the churchyard. Oh lordy! I count three fellas inside. A wave of fear runs through me.

I drop back to the floor and put a finger to my lips. Outside, doors open and slam shut. We hear voices.

"It's Saturday. Ain't nobody here, man." Can always tell a white boy's Southern drawl.

"They might come. Coloreds always go to church when there's trouble."

"Well, they ain't here."

"Just in case, we're gonna wait—and keep our shotgunshandy."

"Hey, what if there was no church for them to come to? They would hate that."

"What you mean?"

"Burn it down. That'll make the neegas weep."

"Burn the church down? That's a good idea. Hey, let's make a party out of it!"

"Might as well. We already got our red shirts on. We look like the ole-timey Red Shirts that Daddy told me about!"

"Yeah. They busted up that love story—white and colored thinking they was gonna run the government together."

"What you talkin' 'bout, Digger?"

"Stuff that happened a long time ago, Mouse. Eighteen ninety-eight. Don't hurt yourself thinkin' 'bout it."

Laughter.

"Will y'all shut up? Let's get a swig and start the party."

"Man! I wish Freight Train was here!"

We hear the doors of the truck open and slam shut again. Then silence.

Me and Mason look at one another. Freight Train's cousins Digger and Mouse are out there!

We Rangers sit quiet, looking at one another...and then all eyes turn to me.

Like always, Skeeter says what everybody's thinking. "Are they really gonna set fire to the church, Cato?"

"I don't know. Maybe they'll just get drunk and go home," I whisper, not even believing my own self.

"Didn't sound like it," says Raymond D. "What're we gonna do?"

I don't answer him, just stretch my legs out and rest my back against the wall. My heart pounds.

All I wanted to do was play that one game!

I can feel the fear rising around me. I can see it in the Rangers' faces. I look away, gazing about the sanctuary instead. I notice things I never have before, like cobwebs in the corners and paint wearing thin on the pews.

It's mighty quiet outside. *Why is it so quiet?*

When the silence goes on longer than I can stand, I get up and peep out of the small window in the door of the church again.

The three fellas are squeezed together in the front seat of the pickup truck again, talking, laughing, and passing a Mason jar between them. White lightning, I reckon. Then I see something that sends my heart racing: a large tin can with a spout sits on the ground next to the truck.

*121*

"Raymond D's right." My voice is low. "They're likkerin' up. And there's a kerosene can on the ground next to the truck."

"They meant what they said, I reckon," mutters Skeeter darkly.

Everybody glares at him.

"Criss-a-mighty, Cato. We can't let this happen," says Mason. "What're we gonna do?"

"We're caught like rats in a trap," mumbles CP.

"We need to get out of here," whispers Skeeter, putting his hands on his face.

"No, Mason's right. We can't let them burn the church down," Hank agrees.

"There's only three of them," Raymond D. whispers. "And we've got guns, too!"

Mason waves his arms. "Fellas, fellas! Rev said not to use those 'less we had no choice. We still got a choice—right, Cato?"

I glance around at all the frightened faces.

"First, we need to get out of here," I tell them. "While they're busy drinking, we can all leave through the back door. Then we'll figure out how to stop them from setting a fire."

"Yeah, we can sneak up on them and…and then what, Cato?" Raymond D. looks puzzled.

"First things first. Everybody outside!"

But before we can make a move, we hear the doors to the truck open and close again.

"I think we ought to start the fire now and drink the other jar while we watch it burn!"

"Ha ha. You're drunk already, Mouse, but that's a pretty good idea."

"This ain't gonna feel as good as smashing some heads, you know."

"We can do that later. I'd love to see 'em bleed the color of these red shirts we've got on."

Laughter.

An icy chill hangs in the air now.

Every Ranger's face shows just what he's thinking. Skeeter looks scared; Raymond D., wild-eyed and ready to fight. And Mason's got a look that I've never seen before. He rubs his chest slowly and stares at the shotguns lying on the pew in back of the church.

"We'd better get going," I whisper firmly. "You move pretty fast, CP. You go out first and the rest of us will follow."

"You and Mason gonna stay in here with the shotguns pointing at the door, right?" suggests Raymond D.

"Yeah. Me and Mason will stand guard, keep them from coming in while you fellas get out through Rev's study."

Lordy. I feel a knot in my stomach now. This is what Rev warned us about, but thought would never happen.

I pick up a shotgun and hand it to Mason. He grips it with both hands, a strange smile on his face.

Hank moves close to me, muttering. "Cato? You sure Mason is the best one to give a shotgun to? Never seen a look like that before."

"Yep. He's the one. Me and Mason are a team," I whisper, picking up the second shotgun.

Hank shakes his head.

Keeping low under the windows, CP starts crawling on his belly toward Rev's sermon room, which has a door to the outside. The Rangers wriggle quickly after him.

As soon as they're gone, a rock crashes into the sanctuary and lands in front of the altar. Me and Mason hold our breath. Glass shatters on the wooden floor, and warm air drifts in through the broken window. We can hear the voices outside more clearly now.

"Why we breaking windows?"

"To get inside the church, silly."

"Why don't we just break down the door?"

"We will, but this is fun! I like the sound of breaking glass."

"Oh. Okay."

A rock crashes through another window. Now there's glass all over the front of the church.

"Kerosene in a jar, and a match. I bet that's what's coming in next," whispers Mason.

I nod. "Let's get out of here."

Me and Mason crawl on our bellies to the sermon room, careful that our shotguns' safety catches are on, careful that we don't step on broken glass. We get outside just as the last window on the right side of the church is shattered.

We join the rest of the Rangers, huddled under a clump of trees. From here we can see what's going on in the churchyard, back and front. The white boys are walking back to where the kerosene is.

Sweat breaks out on my forehead and my underarms. One of the boys is picking up the kerosenecan from the ground now. Another boy grabs a second can from the back of the truck.

"Uh-oh, Cato," says Mason.

I gesture for the Rangers to stay where they are. "Come on," I tell Mason, moving away from the rest.

"What're you doing?" he asks. He's breathing heavy and licking his lips.

"Follow," is all I say.

Me and Mason hurry over to the side of the church, stepping quietly, and inch our way toward the front. The two white boys are still standing near the pickup truck, holding the kerosene cans. The third boy is holding a box of matches in his hand.

My heart pounds. Sweat pours down the small of my back. The only part of me that feels steady is my hands.

I step away from the church wall, raise the shotgun.

Aim.

And fire.

I feel a sudden jerk against my shoulder, then hear the shot.

*Kapow!*

The white boys freeze, crouch downwhere they're standing, and look around wildly, but I've already pressed myself back up next to the church.

"Who dat shooting at us!?"

Before he gets an answer, a second shot rings out.

*Kapow!*

Branches break over the white boys' heads where the shot's scatter cuts them.

I turn and look at Mason, lowering his shotgun as he slams his back against the church. "Criss-a-mighty! Let's get out of here 'fore we kill somebody," he gasps, trembling.

The white boys drop the kerosene cans on the ground. They bump into one another rushing into the pickup truck. Starting the engine with the doors still open, they turn around in a wide circle in the churchyard, then speed off, swerving from one side of the road to the other.

Their truck nearly collides with Rev's. Three more trucks follow his—an army of grown folks come to save us, I reckon.

# Chapter 22

## RETRIBUTION

It's late when Rev brings me home from Saint John's. I'm so hungry I could eat a bear. Gran cooked a special dinner for us—to celebrate if we beat the Marlins, and to ease the pain if we lost. We all sit down at the kitchen table to eat it now.

Rev and Papa Vee describe the awful things that happened at the ball game while I shovel cold fried chicken and potato salad into my mouth. When they're done, I tell what happened at the church: how white boys in red shirts broke the windows and threw rocks, how we thought they were going to set the church on fire, how me and Mason stopped them. Hearing it all nearly sets Rev's hair on fire—his eyes are smoldering. Gran is really troubled when she hears about the white boys throwing rocks through the church windows and figuring to set it on fire.

"Amos? Does this mean we won't have church tomorrow?" she asks.

"Oh, we're having church, Mama J!" Rev pounds his fist on the table, determined. "Might be a little breezy though. The Rangers and the deacons cleaned up as much as possible before we left Saint John's, and we put plywood over the broken windows. Gotta run now. Need to get up early to open up the doors for Sunday school."

Rev kisses Gran on her forehead, gives Papa Vee a pat on the back, and storms out the door.

The weight of the day falls on me suddenly. My shoulders sag, and my eyelids droop.

Gran gets up from her chair, walks over, and hugs me tightly around the neck. "Go on to bed, son. You were a hero today."

---

Next thing I know, I hear Gran and Hope and Papa Vee bustling about in the kitchen. Sunday morning already!

"Cato? You awake?" Hope pulls back the curtain. "You know you don't get to stay home just because you saved the church."

"Ugh," I say, pulling the quilt up over my face.

"You're not the only one who didn't get any sleep," she sniffs.

"*Ugh!*" I roll the quilt back, then pull it over my head again.

"Get *up*, lazybones!" Hope walks away, leaving the curtain wide open. I feel an irritating breeze as somebody opens the back door.

"Hey! Get up, Satch!"

I yank the quilt off my face. Isaac and Philly Dan are standing in the doorway of the pantry, grinning.

"That new windup of yours is coming along nicely," says Philly Dan. "A little more practice and you'll be dangerous."

I shrug. We both know I didn't pitch nearly as well as I wanted to.

Isaac reaches down and flings the quilt off of me completely. "Get up, Cato. You might be a hero, but nobody gets to skip service in this house. You know that."

"I'll go! Just leave me alone."

Isaac and Philly Dan disappear out the back door. By the time I put on my church clothes and my best shoes, I can hear an engine starting. Like last week, everybody's already inside Papa Vee's truck, waiting for me. I run out the door and hop onto the bed of the truck with Isaac and Philly Dan. Hope waves at me from her seat inside between Gran and Papa Vee as we start rolling down the road.

When we get to Saint John's, Rev is already in the pulpit and the congregation is singing their first hymn. As we walk to our pew, a morning breeze rushes in through gaps in the plywood that cover the broken windows.

I'm surprised when everyone stops singing. Someone in the back of the church starts clapping. A few more join in. Then, suddenly, everybody in the whole church is standing and clapping their hands, including Rev.

I freeze. What's going on? Is this for *me*?

Rev raises his hand in the air and the clapping stops. "Well done, my good and faithful servant. Because of you, Cato, we have a church to worship in this morning."

"Amen," the congregation calls out as folks sit down again.

"And I want to say that Saint John's is very proud of the Pender County Rangers. Through all the fighting and confusion these past few weeks, you've shown courage and good judgment. You behaved like men."

"Amen!" shouts the congregation with more applause.

Rev raises his hand for silence, then says, "Stand up, Rangers!"

I stand with the team. We're all looking at one another and around at the church family, grinning and feeling proud. Finally, everybody sits down, and the church is quiet enough for Rev to go on with the morning service.

But it isn't long before Mason's dad, who is ushering today, comes to our row and motions for me and Papa Vee to follow him. Everyone stares as we make our way to the aisle and then the back of the church. Mr. Brown opens the door, and me and Papa Vee step outside.

Trace is standing there, holding his New Hanover Marlins baseball cap in his hands. He nods to us. "Daddy wants to talk to you."

Mr. Luke Blackburn is next to his pickup truck, a little ways away. He's dressed in everyday clothes, which means he didn't go to his own church today. We all walk over to him.

"Morning, Vernon," says Mr. Luke.

"Mornin', Luke."

"Heard about what happened here last night. Mighty sorry—but proud of your boys."

"Yep. Seems a few white boys slipped past the men we had watching out for trouble."

"Hate to tell you this, Vernon, but from what I hear, trouble's still a-stirring."

"Yep." Papa Vee looks down at the ground for a moment, then back at Mr. Luke. "Harlee Jamison found a cross burning in his front yard last night."

"And I hear that some of those responsible are looking for Cato now," says Mr. Luke. "I reckon striking out all the Marlins batters in one inning was too much for them."

"Or they just had enough of white and colored baseball," says Papa Vee. "We'd better go ahead with our plan, Luke."

Mr. Luke nods. Me and Trace look at one another, puzzled.

Papa Vee puts both hands on my shoulders and looks at me directly. "Son, I want you to go with Luke. Your grandma packed you a satchel. It's already in his truck. Should only be a few days 'fore all this dies down."

"Let's hope no more than a week, for sure," says Mr. Luke.

"A week? I'm going to live with him for a *week*?"

"Not live with him. You'll sleep in his hayloft."

My mouth is dry and my head is spinning. I'm so confused. Last night, the Rangers showed we can stand up to trouble, not run away from it.

"But Papa Vee, we stopped those white boys from burning down the church. We fought back! I don't want to run from them now!" I'm trying to keep my voice low, trying to keep from getting mad and disrespecting him again.

"You heard what Luke said. They've singled you out, son. They were scared that if you kept pitching good, the Rangers would win the game. And I bet they know you're the Rangers captain and the one who shot at the boys at the church last night."

"Were the fellas at the church last night wearing red?" asks Mr. Luke.

"Yes," I say. I think about telling him that Digger and Mouse were there, but I don't. Colored folks don't go 'round pointing fingers at whites.

"These boys remind me of the Red Shirts from long ago, Luke," says Papa Vee grimly.

"One of the boys last night talked about Red Shirts, Papa Vee. What are they?" I ask.

"Colored and whites banded together in 1898 to run for office in Wilmington: some were Republicans, some were Populists. It was called Fusion. Their Fusion people were elected—as mayor, aldermen, police chief. But white folks in the Democratic party didn't like it. So they run all of 'em outta town. With rifles at their backs. The dirty work was done by the Red Shirts."

"You know, Vernon, for a long time, they called that mess in 1898 a race riot," says Mr. Luke.

"Yep. But weren't no riot. It was more like a war. Those men was run outta town with a shotgun at their backs."

Mr. Luke frowns, takes his hat off, scratches the top of his head, then puts it back on. His face looks like he just bit into a lemon. "Have mercy, Vernon. Don't like to be reminded of Carolina's sorry history."

Papa Vee gazes at me. Like always, he seems calm and determined, not worried at all. "I know you don't want to go, son…know it seems like running away to you…but a man's got to know when to be strong, and when to be smart."

I raise both arms in the air, not ready to give up. "But Papa Vee—"

Papa Vee raises his voice just enough. "Cato. I'm not asking you, son, I'm telling you."

I bite down hard on my lower lip to hold back the anger and the tears. "Yes suh," I say.

"Go on with Luke now."

Papa Vee hugs me tight for just a moment, then turns and walks back toward the church. As I watch him move away from me, it takes all the strength I've got to keep from running after him.

# Chapter 23
## HAYLOFT

I climb into Mr. Luke's truck in between him and Trace. There's not much room for the three of us, and pretty soon my left leg is sore from being hit every time Mr. Luke shifts gears. Me and Trace bump shoulders as the truck bounces.

I dig my fingernails into my arm. Lordy. What am I doing sitting between these white folks? Everything that happened since the Rangers first went to Poplar Field seems like a bad dream. That was so long ago. Before then, all I had to think about was baseball.

"Well, this didn't turn out the way I hoped it would," says Mr. Luke. He stares at the road, like he's talking to his own self. "Could say it turned out gosh-awful, but you boys should know that it was important for you to do this."

Me and Trace look at one another. From Trace's expression, I know he's thinking what I'm thinking. Neither of us agrees.

"We made history, boys. Your teams played against one another. Mo and I could never do that." Mr. Luke sounds like he did when me and Papa Vee went calling on him at his store, like he's thinking about old times. Then, all a sudden, his voice sounds really different. "Cato? I want you to slide down to the floor, very, very slowly. Do it now, son."

I do what Mr. Luke tells me. Just before my head goes below the dashboard, I glance out the windshield and see a car coming toward us. Trace moves his legs closer to the door to give me room, and I curl up in a ball on the floor. All I hear is the hum of the engine, but boy, I can feel my heart pounding and I'm starting to sweat.

"Whew! It turned," says Trace.

"Don't get up yet, Cato," says Mr. Luke. "Somebody could still be watching us."

"Yes suh," I say, breathing in the hot air on the floor of the truck.

After a while, Mr. Luke's truck turns onto a side road and stops. "Stay down until I tell you to move, Cato." Mr. Luke gets out, leaving the door open. He goes around to the back and, I think, grabs my satchel.

A moment later he's back, motioning to me with his hands. "Come now! Quickly! To the barn."

I slide across the driver's seat, under the steering wheel, and hop down onto the ground, then run for the open barn door. Trace appears beside me, matching me step for step.

When we get inside, we wait for Mr. Luke. He closes the barn door behind him when he arrives. "You can settle in now, Cato. We'll be back later. Your grandma put some lunch in the satchel for you."

"Yes suh," I say, taking the satchel out of Mr. Luke's hand.

I look around, see the ladder to the hayloft, and start to climb it.

At the top of the ladder, I lift the satchel up first, put my knee onto the floor of the hayloft, and crawl in. It's mighty clean up here. Nothing but baling wire, a few sacks of seed, and what's left of the hay from last winter. In our loft, you would find a stray chicken or two, some squirrels, or a bird's nest.

I gather up enough hay to make myself a bed and grab a burlap sack from the corner to make a pillow. Then I lie down and close my eyes.

Still don't know how I feel about firing a shotgun at somebody or hiding out in Mr. Luke's barn like a coward.

I'm tired though. It's not surprising that I drift off to sleep. It was the nap I would've gotten in church while Rev was preaching.

———

I'm not sure how long I slept, but the sound of voices startles me. Trace is coming into the barn, and he's not alone.

"What do you think you're doing, Freight Train? You can't just go anywhere you want on our property!"

I hold my breath. Then, quiet as I can, I inch my way to the back of the hayloft so a body would have to climb the ladder to the top to see me.

"First off, we got no business playing baseball with colored boys. And if we do, we need to beat the stuffin' out of 'em—teach them a lesson."

"Marlins probably would've beat them if we played a full game," insists Trace.

"Well, I don't like having Marlins struck out by colored boys. Their pitcher, that Cato fella, needs to be whupped upside the head. Or worse."

"Stop talking like that! It's just baseball. Marlins aren't going to gang up on a fella just because he's a good pitcher."

"*Just baseball?* Have you lost your mind, Trace? We've got to keep them coloreds in their place, no matter what."

"Look, man, Marlins aren't looking to fight anybody. Besides, Daddy would never hear of it. You and your cousin need to go on home now."

"Well, since we're here, what say we have a look around, see if this Cato fella is around. Nobody's seen the little critter, so maybe he snuck in here without you knowing." Freight Train takes a few steps closer to the ladder that leads to the hayloft. Then I hear the barn door open again.

"What's going on?" asks Mr. Luke. "Freight Train? What're you boys doing here?"

"Just visitin', Mr. Luke. This is my cousin, Digger, from South Carolina."

"Yes, I saw Digger at the game," says Mr. Luke coldly. "You're the one that made that gawd-awful noise before everything just went to hell."

"That was a rebel yell, suh. My daddy taught me that," says Digger proudly.

"The Civil War is over," says Mr. Luke, his voice hard. "You boys need to leave now. We're about to have dinner."

"Yes suh, Mr. Luke," says Freight Train, but he doesn't sound too polite. "We'll see you at the ball field, Trace."

Feet shuffle. The barn door closes. Then all is quiet.

I lay still, my heart beating fast.

After a while, my stomach starts to rumble. Mr. Luke and Trace must be eating that dinner he talked about.

I reach for my satchel, open it, and see a brown paper sack and a Mason jar half full of water right on top. My lunch! My face breaks out in a smile. *Thanks, Gran!*

I put the sack in my lap, pull out a ham biscuit, and take a big bite. Didn't know I was so hungry. After eating and taking a big swig of water from the Mason jar, I lay down, close my eyes, and drift off into another fitful sleep.

I dream that I'm in the woods, being chased by a bear, and he's gaining on me...

I wake up all a sudden when the barn door creaks open. It's dusk-dark, and the memory of the nightmare still lingers.

"Cato, it's me."

I peek over the side of the loft and see Trace carrying a tin of food in one hand and a lantern in the other. A blanket is thrown over his shoulder.

He sets the lamp down on the floor and steps on the lowest rung of the ladder, balancing the tin in one hand and holding on with the other. I place my hands on the ladder to steady it, letting go when he gets to the top. Trace puts the pie pan in front of me, climbs back down to fetch the lantern, then comes into the loft. He lays the blanket on the floor and sits down facing me, knees drawn up to his chest, arms wrapped around them. The single lantern casts an eerie glow on us.

I sit cross-legged, pull the blanket into my lap, lay the pie pan on top of it, and start eating. Collard greens, sweet potatoes, cornbread. I bite down on the biggest pork chop I've ever seen.

"Daddy told me what happened after the game," says Trace slowly. "How you boys hid out in your church, and some fellas broke windows and were aiming to set it on fire."

I don't say a word, just look at Trace as I chomp down on the tasty pork chop.

"Heard you ran those fellas off with shotguns too. That must have been something!"

I nod, shoving some candied sweet potato into my mouth. All I can think about now is how good the food is. Trace's mother is almost as good a cook as Gran.

Trace stares at me for a moment, then laughs. "Can't find your tongue? Mama cooks pretty good, huh?"

I smile with my mouth full, then lick my fingers.

Trace smiles and pats his stomach. "I saw your brother at the game. Looks like he's all better now. It's creepy how much the two of you look alike."

"What?" I say after I swallow. "I do not look like Isaac!"

"Do too. What position does he play?"

"He pitches for the Kansas City Monarchs."

"The who?"

"The Kansas City Monarchs of the Negro American League."

"Oh. Yeah. I've heard Daddy talk about colored teams."

"My daddy played with the Kansas City Monarchs too, just like Isaac."

Trace's cheeks turn red. Mr. Luke must have told him that Daddy Mo is dead. "Are you going to play with the Monarchs too?"

"Yep. Soon as Papa Vee says I can go to Kansas City. Feels like they're holding a place for the next pitcher in the Jones family."

"Man!" says Trace, his eyes beaming. "I wish I had a beeline to a professional baseball team too."

"Yeah? Which one?"

"I'd pitch for the Chicago Cubs."

"Somebody had better tell Dizzy Dean that you're coming for his job." We both laugh.

"Well, are you going to take Isaac's job when you join the Monarchs?"

I laugh out loud. "No! Isaac will still be on the mound when I get there. I'll prob'ly sit on the bench or be a relief pitcher. The Monarchs have Satchel Paige, anyway. He's the greatest pitcher who ever lived. Him and Isaac are good friends."

"Are you crazy? The greatest pitcher who ever lived is named Dizzy Dean."

"Isaac and Philly Dan have seen both of them pitch, and they say Satchel is better."

"You're dreaming! This Paige fella must be like you, thinking he's the best in the world, no matter what."

"Well, if the shoe fits." I shrug.

"So, what's with this windup of yours, raising your leg high in the air like that? Seemed like you started that in the fifth inning, and that's when you struck all of us out."

"Hey, I was trying to do it from the very first inning." I shake my head. "Started doing that windup a year ago. Helps me throw the ball harder and faster."

"Man, I'd lose my balance and fall if I tried that," says Trace.

"If I keep it up, I might too," I say, laughing. "But for now, it works for me."

Trace pulls two pieces of licorice out of his pocket, shoving one in my direction. I shake my head, preferring the square of cornbread on my plate.

"I'm going to Kansas City with Isaac this summer," I say. "Gonna meet Satchel Paige and watch him pitch an all-star game."

Trace's eyes get big. "Man! I wouldn't mind going with you."

I stare at him as I finish eating my cornbread. "Maybe," I say.

I look away from Trace, then bite down on my lower lip. Who ever heard of a white boy going to an all-star game of a colored team?

# Chapter 24
## CONFESSION

When I first got here, I thought that living in Mr. Luke's barn was going to be the worst thing that ever happened to me.

I was wrong. It's been kind of fun.

Me and Trace worked on the engine of the old pickup truck that me and Mason unloaded at the store. And I've spent hours looking at Trace's baseball cards, wishing that we had cards for Negro League players. I'd get twenty cards for Satchel Paige. No, a hundred!

Me and Trace also play catch inside the barn every day, but I miss practicing with the Rangers and hurling that ball as hard as I can to strike out a batter. And I'm ready to see Gran, Hope, Papa Vee, Isaac, and Rev. Philly Dan, too. Mason, especially, and even Moses the kitty.

"Cato? You awake?"

It's early morning but I'm up. Trace is carrying a pie pan in each hand stacked high with hoecakes, sausage links, and a bottle of Karo syrup. He sets them on the table I made from two barrels I found in the barn. I climb down from the hayloft to join him.

"That's a mighty big stack of hoecakes," I say. "If you can't eat all of yours—"

"I can eat them," says Trace, "but I'll have a piece of your sausage if you get too full." Trace grins, shoves a forkful of hoecakes and syrup into his mouth, and takes a big bite of sausage.

We both put our heads down and don't look up until we're done. Then we turn the pie pans up to our faces and lick the syrup off the bottom.

"Your mama's hoecakes are almost as good as my grandma's," I admit.

"Yeah? Next time she makes some, I'll have to come and see."

I look at Trace. The thought of him sitting at our kitchen table eating hoecakes would have seemed strange a few days ago, but not now.

Mr. Luke comes inside the barn. "Soon as you boys finish eating, it'll be time for you to go home, Cato."

"Yes suh!" I say, surprised. But lordy, I'm ready!

I rush up to the hayloft and throw my belongings into Isaac's satchel. When I come back down, I hurry for the door, waving at Trace on my way out.

I throw the satchel in the back and hop into the cab. Somehow it seems small and cramped, like there's not enough air. I glance sideways. Been around Mr. Luke a lot these past four days, but it's strange to be so close to him. In spite of all he's done to keep me safe, I still don't know how I feel about him.

Mr. Luke backs the truck out of his yard, and we head for the place I call home.

"You know, Cato, watching you on the ball field reminds me so much of your father," says Mr. Luke. "He was a great pitcher—the best I've ever seen."

I can't help but smile when I hear this. "Did you and Daddy Mo play baseball together when you were growing up?"

"In a match, never. Back then, things were the same as now. Colored players couldn't be on white teams, and we didn't play games against each other either. But I practiced with the Cyclones sometimes—that was Mo's team—and Mo and I hit balls back and forth every day, for training."

"Every day?" My eyes get wide now, but I can't let Mr. Luke see.

"Every day. Did your grandpa ever tell you any stories about that?"

"No."

Mr. Luke takes his eyes off the road for a moment to look at me. His forehead is wrinkled, the corners of his mouth turned down.

"Then I'll tell you some things about what life was like for Mo and me." Mr. Luke pauses for a moment and takes in a deep breath. "My daddy had four brothers. Not one of them had a head for business, so your grandpa helped Daddy keep the books for our farm. And because Vernon was at our house every day, Mo was there too. We both loved baseball and played all of the time."

I gaze at Mr. Luke. I'm a little uneasy with this white man, even now, but I want to know everything about Daddy Mo's life.

"Moses was the best pitcher for miles around, white or colored. We all knew he could be on a major league team if they allowed it. But they didn't. So he went to play on a Negro League team instead. I got to see the Kansas City Monarchs play a few times. They were just as good as any major league white team I ever saw. Maybe better."

My chest swells with pride when I hear this. I turn sideways in my seat, leaning in closer to Mr. Luke, wanting to hear every word he has to say.

"Mo went to Kansas City when he was seventeen, and I stayed here to help Daddy with the farm. We wrote some letters back and forth, and I'd see him when I went to his games in Kansas City or when he came home. Your grandma had a birthday dinner for him every year and I was always invited."

My mouth drops. *Mr. Luke* was invited to Daddy Mo's birthday dinners?

"When Mo died, I stopped going to see Vernon and Miss Nina. It just hurt too much to be at that house, knowing that Mo wasn't ever going to be there again. Some Colored people thought that I had something to do with his death, I reckon. Thought I could have stopped what happened, or at least found the men who did it. Colored folks stopped coming into my store. Amos certainly blames me. I never said anything to defend myself, because I blame me too. If I had done just one thing different, Mo might be alive today."

My heart almost stops when I hear this.

What could Mr. Luke have done differently that would have made Daddy Mo live? *One thing?*

My stomach turns upside down as I wait for Mr. Luke to go on talking, but he doesn't say another word. Instead, he lets out a long sigh, grips the steering wheel tight with both hands, and shakes his head. I don't know what to think, what to feel.

I ball up a fist and press it hard into my stomach so I can keep those hoecakes down.

Thoughts of Daddy Mo and Mr. Luke playing baseball when they were young swirl through my head...but then I see a house full of people with a casket in the front room.

I'm eight years old. Papa Vee is standing by the casket. A kerchief covers his whole face. His shoulders shake, but no sound comes out of him. I run to him and put my hand on his arm. He wipes his face, scoops me up in his arms, my legs dangling, and hugs me tight. My head is resting on Papa Vee's shoulder when I look up and see Rev in the kitchen, his head buried in Gran's bosom.

I felt scared and sick that day. Hearing what Mr. Luke just said—those feelings are coming back now.

We're halfway home when Mr. Luke starts talking again. "You know, Cato, I loved your daddy, and I love your family. Until Mo died, I never knew that life could be so bright one minute and turn so dark the next. I'm just glad to be in your life again, glad that you and Trace will get to know one another. Mo is looking down on us now and smiling."

What Mr. Luke says sends chills all through me. Never *ever* would have thought that he could be so close to the people I love.

Mr. Luke smiles, but it fades quickly, and he looks sad again.

"A man like me has got no right to ask for forgiveness, especially of a boy as young as you, Cato. So I won't do that. But I want you to know that I'm looking for—no, praying for—the day when my name crosses your lips in the spirit of forgiveness. Forgiveness for the things that I didn't do."

Tears roll down Mr. Luke's cheeks. He takes out a white kerchief and wipes his face.

The sight of this grown man crying scares me. It scares me even more than the sad memories in my head. But I want to know more.

"Mr. Luke? What did you mean…when you said that Daddy Mo might be alive if you had done something different?"

Mr. Luke takes his eyes off the road for a moment to look at me. "Son, didn't Vernon or your grandma tell you about that day? Tell you what happened to Mo, or why some people blame me?"

"No suh."

"My, my, my! Wouldn't have said what I did if I had known."

We stop talking for a little while.

"It's not my place to say anything more, Cato. You ought to talk to Vernon, son. Talk to Vernon."

"Yes suh." I turn toward the window and let my own tears roll down my cheeks.

My mouth is dry, and my chest is tight. Still can't figure out how I'm s'posed to feel about Mr. Luke. Should I be mad at him for something he didn't do, something he won't even talk about? Should I pity him? Hate him? Rev said I shouldn't, even though he does himself.

But there's one thing I do know. He must have loved Daddy Mo a lot. Losing him still hurts.

# Chapter 25
## TRUTH
——

There's a crowd in the front yard when me and Mr. Luke drive up to the house. Everyone I care about is here: Papa Vee, Gran, Hope, Isaac, Rev, the Rangers, and Philly Dan. Even Nate and Ollie have come. I hop out of the truck and grab my satchel from the back.

Gran rushes up to me ahead of anybody else. "Lord a mercy! You look thin, Cato. Did that woman feed you?"

"Yes'm. She fed me good."

Gran blows out a long breath. "If you say so. I've got a mess of greens cooked and we're having fried chicken for supper."

"But it's not Sunday," I say, surprised.

"You've come home, son. That makes today special." Gran kisses me on my forehead and I don't pull away, even though the Rangers are watching.

Behind me, Papa Vee walks over to Mr. Luke's truck and leans in. They talk for a while, then Mr. Luke revs up the truck and drives away.

Everybody welcomes me home in their own way. Hope rushes into my arms and hugs me, then steps back and gives me the brightest smile. Isaac puts his arms around me, embracing me lightly like a brother would. Philly Dan shakes my hand while patting me on the back at the same time. Nate and Ollie stand off to the side of the yard and just grin and wave.

Then the Rangers gather 'round me and take turns slapping me on the back. Each one hits me harder than the last one did. I'm laughing, but after a while, my back starts to hurt.

"We want to know everything that happened," says Mason. "Don't leave nothing out."

"Well, first off, I stayed in the hayloft in Mr. Luke's barn—"

"*The hayloft?*" Hank and Raymond D. say at the same time.

I shake my head. "How you think it would look if a colored boy all a sudden moved in with Mr. Luke? Folks would talk—and the Rebel Clan would surely hear aboutit!"

"Oh," says Hank. "Is that what we're calling them? Rebel Clan?"

I tell the Rangers pretty much everything, and I make it sound like Mr. Luke treated me real special. I talk a lot about the pork chops, sausage, and hoecakes, and about Trace's baseball cards.

Gran brings out two apple pies, some cups, and a pitcher of lemonade. Talking dies down while we shovel pie into our mouths and gulp down cold, sweet lemonade.

"They burned a cross in my yard while you were gone, and one in Deacon Jamison's yard a few days ago," says Smokey Joe. "Must've been some fellas too dumb to be in the real Klan though. The cross was only two feet tall and the fire went out as soon as they drove off."

We all laugh, but we know it's not funny.

———

I've been home hours now. Gran comes out onto the front porch, her arms folded over her chest. The look on her face says the Rangers need to leave.

"Um, fellas, I'm sort of tired," I lie. "I'll see you all at Walker Field tomorrow."

"You don't look tired," says Skeeter, narrowing his eyes.

"Cuz, will you just come on," says Raymond D., pulling him by the arm. "You see the look on Miss Nina's face!"

When all the Ranger have gone, Gran sits down in the swing on the front porch. I sit beside her.

"Sounds like Luke treated you pretty good. We sure don't see many pork chops around here," says Gran, smiling. "Now, there was a time when

I used to cook for Sheriff Pridgeon's daddy and his family. Then there was plenty of meat here every day."

"What? Tell me about that, Gran."

Gran smiles so wide her eyes crinkle, and her dimples show. "Hmm. There's a lot of things about the old days that I need to tell you. Some other time."

"Yes'm." I sit way back and tap my foot on the porch so the swing starts to move.

"I know that you and your grandpa have had some words about you going to Kansas City with Isaac when he leaves. Circumstance has changed all that now." Gran puts her hand on mine and pats it three times. "We don't know when Isaac will be going back.

"Cato, Vernon said you asked him to tell you about Mo—how he died, and what Luke had to do with it." Gran lets her words hang in the air for a moment. "Son, your grandpa can't talk to you about that. Brave as he is, his heart would just break in two if he tried. He asked me to talk to you instead."

"Yes'm." My heart starts pounding. Now that the moment is here, I'm scared of what Gran will say.

Gran folds her hands in her lap, her fingers knitted together like always when she's studying on something. She taps the floor and makes the swing go a little faster.

"Life seems ord'nary most days, but every now and again something happens that you just can't explain. It was like that on the day your daddy died.

"It was a Saturday, two days before Mo's birthday. We were expecting him to come home from Kansas City. I was making a chocolate cake, like I always do, and Vernon was fixing things around the farm with Nate and Ollie. We were all beside ourselves with happiness, but when Mo hadn't got here by two o'clock, we started to worry. He should've got off the bus from Wilmington at noon.

"'Round three o'clock, Luke come by asking where Mo was—said he was supposed to pick him up at the bus stop, but he didn't get there on time. Said he couldn't find Mo anywhere. Luke thought that Mo might've walked home, but he wasn't here.

"Well, the men went looking for Mo then. Your grandpa, Amos, Luke, and Harlee Jamison. As they were going 'round to folks' houses, they found out there was big trouble over in New Hanover County, and it was spilling into Pender County. A bunch of white boys were going 'round dragging colored men out of their homes or out of their trucks and beating them. Your grandpa knew that this was a bad sign. They kept looking for Mo until it was pitch-dark, and then they all came here to wait for daybreak so they could go out again. But...

"Around ten o'clock at night, Sheriff Pridgeon came by the house and called Vernon out to his truck. Vernon went, along with Amos, Harlee, and Luke. I was standing in the door, watching them. The sheriff led them to the back of his truck, turned his flashlight on, and lifted up a black tarp. Your grandpa raised both arms in the air and yelled, 'Lord, no!' That's all he said 'fore he turned and walked back to the porch and straight into my arms.

"That was pretty near the last bit of talking Vernon did for almost a month. Oh, he went to the funeral and all, but he spoke only a few words, and only when he had to. The only times he cried was when the sheriff first brought Mo home on the back of that truck—and at the wake when we brought Mo's casket into the front room."

"But Gran," I ask slowly, "nobody's ever said *how* Daddy Mo died. Did those white boys find him and . . . and beat him so bad that he died from it? Why were they beating up colored men anyway?"

"The way it started was kind of silly, though I reckon it made sense to the small-minded boys who were doing it. A little white girl went into the woods near her church. She fell into a hole that was dug to catch a bear somebody thought they saw roaming around. Instead of every able-bodied man looking for her, some of them listened to gossip and wild talk instead. Somebody heard that somebody said they saw a colored man running into the woods carrying a little white girl. So, a mess o' white boys went around beating up colored men, even though it wasn't helping to find that little girl. But there was one bunch of boys that was worse than the rest. They wanted to do more than just beat people."

Gran stops talking and gathers the bottom of her apron into her hands. A few tears roll down her cheeks. Her voice is low, barely above a whisper when she continues.

"Somebody had a rope in the back of his truck. And there are plenty of sturdy trees in New Hanover County. So, they threw one end of the rope over the branch of a big ole oak tree, and put the other end around my son's neck…"

I gasp! Then stand straight up. Oh my lordy!

My hands fly up to my face. The swing is still moving, and it bangs into the back of my legs. I turn and face Gran, breathing hard, but she can't see me. The hem of her apron covers her face, and her shoulders shake.

Seeing Gran like this scares me—makes me want to make things right again. Slowly, I sit back down in the swing and pull her gently into my arms.

We sit quietly, swinging back and forth, until she stops crying.

"We didn't mean to wait so long to tell you, Cato. It's just so hard to say the words. Your grandpa couldn't say them, and I can barely get them out."

Gran looks at me, then draws my head onto her bosom and sets the swing to moving again. She rubs circles on my back, like she always has when she knows I'm hurting.

I think about the kitty cat, Moses, and how Freight Train and his cousins tortured him. How he fought mightily. Is that how it was for Daddy Mo? Did he fight mightily too? And lose?

The tears come in waves, nearly choking me. I can barely catch my breath. Spit drools out of my mouth and rolls onto Gran's dress. My nose runs too.

Though it's been there all my life, I have never let myself feel the hurt like this.

When the crying slows and Gran is sure I can breathe, she pulls away from me and looks into my eyes. "We are not going to remember Mo for how he died. We're going to celebrate who he was and how he lived. That's why we have a dinner on his birthday every year. Can't nothing take away the pain of how we lost him, Cato, but every time you smile, or eat a molasses biscuit, or pitch a baseball game, you honor his life."

Papa Vee has prob'ly kept everybody away from the porch, 'cause nobody's come outside for a long time. Me and Gran sit there for an hour or more, hugging one another, swinging back and forth and listening to the crickets sing.

# Chapter 26
## THE POSTCARD

It's been more'n a month since the baseball game between the Rangers and the Marlins was broken up by the Rebel Clan. Excitement about the game has pretty much died down, and nobody even talks about it now. Everybody's relieved that it's over, except for Mr. Luke, maybe. He still hangs onto the dream that me and Trace will be friends like him and Daddy Mo.

The Rangers have a game next week with the Burgaw Barons, a Tidewater Colored League team, but I'm not looking forward to it. Not really. My spirit's mighty low. Finding out how Daddy Mo died has made me so sad.

And seeing white boys acting like the Red Shirts from long ago has made me so mad.

"We need a party," says Isaac one day. We're all sitting on the front porch, drinking the tart lemonade that Gran and Hope just made.

With what I'm feeling—half sad, half mad—I'm not so sure, but I ask, "Should we have Daddy Mo's memorial dinner, then?"

"No. What you and the Rangers need is a *party*. You fellas have been moping around lately and playing some sorry baseball. You all lost a practice game to the Castle Hayne Hornets, for goodness' sake!"

"Isaac's right," says Philly Dan. "The way the Rangers are playing now, you'll never win the Tidewater Colored League championship."

"I can help Gran make pies for a party," says Hope, appearing on the porch. "My sweet potato pie is almost as good as hers."

That cheers me up some. I lick my lips before saying, "Whoa! I can taste that pie right now. Get in the kitchen, girl!"

"All right!" Hope sticks her tongue out at me. "Let's do it tomorrow. I'll tell Gran."

The next day I spread the word at baseball practice, and by late afternoon, the Rangers start coming by the house. Hank and Smokey Joe are the first ones to walk into the front yard.

"Where's Isaac?" asks Hank. "I want to hear some stories about Josh Gibson. Some say he's better'n Babe Ruth, you guys heard that?"

"Don't worry," I say. "Getting Isaac to go on and on about baseball is the easiest thing in the world."

Seems the Rangers aren't the only ones who heard that Gran was making pies. Mason's daddy, Nate, Ollie, and Harlee Junior are here, too. The extra pretty dress Hope is wearing is for Harlee, I reckon.

Gran got some help from the church ladies and there's a full dinner being laid out on a picnic table set under a sycamore tree. (Nate and Ollie built it yesterday.) There's fried chicken, green beans, potato salad, biscuits, and apple and sweet potato pies.

Trace and Mr. Luke show up, too. Since the game, they've come 'round a lot, dropping by on Sundays after supper to eat a piece of Gran's apple pie. Mr. Luke loves to talk about the good old days and tell stories about things that he and Daddy Mo used to do. When Rev's around, though, he never mentions any of that. He's waiting for the preacher in Rev to show some forgiveness, I reckon.

When it's time to eat, we gather 'round the table so Rev can say grace.

"Where's Skeeter and Raymond D.?" asks Hope.

'Fore I can answer, Skeeter and Raymond D. come tearing into the yard.

"What's the matter, son? Somebody chasing you boys?" asks Rev.

Skeeter is panting and out of breath. "No suh. We just wanted to get here before all the food was gone!"

Everybody laughs.

"First thing," says Rev, "you're the last ones to get here. Second thing, you know Mama J never runs out of food!"

Soon everybody's got a plate and found a place for themselves, sitting at the table or on the porch or standing in the yard. The mountain of food is disappearing fast.

Hank gets his wish. Isaac sits in the swing with the Rangers crowded 'round and starts telling stories about the colored baseball players he's met, like always. Pretty soon he's telling tales about the best pitcher who ever lived, Satchel Paige.

Man! I was counting on meeting him this summer, but I'm stuck in Pender County now.

"Mailman's coming!" yells Hope, pointing at a car stopped at our mailbox. "I'll get it."

"I'll race you," says Harlee Junior.

The two of them take off running across the yard. When they get there, Hope opens the box and pulls out something small. She and Harlee Junior look at one another, then bend down and peep into the mailbox again, their heads touching. They walk back to the house slowly, talking to one another.

We almost never get mail, and when we do, it's usually some kind of bad news. Like somebody died or forgot to pay a bill or something.

"It's a postcard for you, Isaac," says Hope. "From someplace in California."

"Who asked you to read my mail, missy?"

"It's a postcard! Anybody that looks at it can read it." Hope laughs.

"Gimme!" says Isaac, getting up.

Hope dashes off, and he chases her around the yard. Isaac finally grabs the postcard out of her hand, lifting her off the ground, both of them laughing. Then he settles back into the porch swing to read it. Everyone stares at him and waits.

Isaac holds up the postcard so everyone can see the front of it. "Now this is a pretty ball field," he says. "I'll pass it around in a minute."

"Son, who's it from?" asks Papa Vee.

"The one and only Satchel Paige, Papa Vee. We write back and forth sometimes when he's on the road. And he's on the road a lot." Isaac laughs.

"Spit it out, Isaac," says Philly Dan. "What does the man say?"

Isaac clears his throat loudly, then reads the lines written on the back of the postcard.

Dear Isaac,

Heard you had some trouble down South. Get better soon now. Ya hear? Can't wait to see you back in Kansas City. Can't wait to tell you 'bout all my adventures in California last winter. Played against the white boys and I outpitched Dizzy Dean. Twice! So, who's the best pitcher in baseball? Satchel Paige, that's who! Hope your little brother gets to play ball in a world that's more like California than Carolina. Ask your grandma to start praying on it right now. Well, take care, li'l brother. Who knows, I just might see you soon.

Satchel

"Dizzy Dean?" yells Trace. "The Cubs are a major league team! How could Satchel Paige be playing baseball with him?"

"That's what they do in the California Winter League," says Philly Dan.

"How's that?" I ask.

"Well," says Isaac, "out in California, white and colored teams play against one another in the offseason. The white teams often include players from Major League Baseball teams."

"What?" the Rangers yell all together.

Trace's eyebrows shoot up. "And colored players are beating white players? That's surprising."

"No it's not, son," says Mr. Luke. "I've told you. There's plenty of Negro League players good enough to play in the major leagues if the law allowed."

Gran walks up the porch steps and stands next to the swing where Isaac is sitting. "My son Moses was good enough to be on a major league team," she says proudly. "And my grandson is too!"

"Any team," agrees Rev.

Trace's eyes drop, and then he looks at me sideways.

"So, while we're futzing around down here, white and colored are playing baseball together in California?" asks Rev.

"Yep," says Isaac. Philly Dan nods too.

"My goodness!" says Gran. "Mr. Paige asked me to pray for a different world for Cato to play baseball in. Been doing that all along."

Rev brings his hand up to his face and scratches his chin. "Reckon it's 'bout time for me to join you, Mama J."

In my mind's eye, I can see Mr. Satchel in California outpitching Dizzy Dean. Then I see myself all growed up, pitching for a major league team myself somewhere. White and black players together.

A different world.

"So how long you and Gran plan on praying 'fore this might happen?" I ask.

Silence. Gran and Rev look down at the ground. Everybody else looks at me.

"Well, now, that's a darned good question if I ever heard one," says Isaac, smiling and shaking his head.

I stare real hard at the other team captain in the yard. "Trace?"

Trace drops his head, looks sideways at Mr. Luke, then turns in my direction. "Guess Mr. Satchel wants us to be like him."

"Yep," I say. "Wants us to make some history down here in Carolina."

Me and Trace gaze at one another. Our chests swell with pride and we raise our fists in the air.

"Right now," we say at the same time. "

———

"Well, I'll be!" both Rev and Mr. Luke whisper under their breaths.

"Um, Cato?" Skeeter steps up in front of me and Trace. "Does that mean that the Rangers and Marlins are gonna play some *more* ball games?"

"Yep," I say simply.

"But Tidewater Colored League ball is more fun. And who's gonna keep them white boys from beating us upOr tryin' to?"

Papa Vee steps up next to Skeeter. "That's just what I was thinking, Skeeter. Glad you said it out loud." Then Papa Vee turns toward Mr. Luke. "What could Sheriff Pridgeon do to make this happen, Luke?"

"Deputies, Vernon. He could swear in a lot of deputies to keep the peace."

"Would you ask him to do that?"

"You know I will. Rev...would you come with me when I do that?"

There's a pause.

"Yes, Luke," Rev says, looking right at him. "I'll come with you.."

Isaac stands up, raises his arms over his head, and claps his hands. "Congratulations, folks. We agreed that the Rangers and the Marlins will play another game. But what happens after that? Is that it?"

Philly Dan winks at me. "I'll give you a hint what he means, Cato. What happens at the end of every baseball season?"

"The World Series!" yells Skeeter.

"And how do we decide who plays in the World Series?" asks Isaac. "Anybody *but* Skeeter," he adds, laughing.

"There's playoffs," I say. "And before the playoffs, division series and stuff."

"Riiight!" says Philly Dan.

"So...you think the Rangers and the Marlins should play a *series* of games?" asks Trace.

Isaac and Philly Dan cross their arms and smile.

"Yes!" Rangers yell all at once.

"And what we gonna call these games?" asks Isaac.

"The Pender County–New Hanover Games!" I say, looking right at Trace.

"Done!" he says, smiling at me.

# Chapter 27
## KINDRED SPIRITS

The Rangers will play the New Hanover Marlins at Poplar Field in two weeks. Both teams will have the chance to win the series we're calling the Pender County–New Hanover Games. Sheriff Pridgeon even promised that he and his deputies would keep an eye open for mischief.

Trace said he had a time trying to get the Marlins to agree to the games. Freight Train didn't want anything to do with the Rangers—or any other colored baseball players. Then Trace told him about the California Winter League and how Satchel Paige outpitched Dizzy Dean in a game that his team won. Had to call in Mr. Luke to say the story was true. Then Mr. Luke shamed the Marlins by saying that they could prob'ly beat the Rangers in one or two games, but if they played five games against us, they just might lose the series. Wish I could've been there to hear the howling when he said that. None of them could imagine losing!

These days, Rangers are spending all of our time at Walker Field, practicing. We know how good the Marlins are now, so we have to play better this time. Smokey Joe, Raymond D., and Hank are waiting in the lineup and the rest of the team is in position on the field. 'Fore I can step onto the mound though, something catches my eye.

Skeeter sees it too. "Jumping jackrabbits!" he yells. "Who's driving that fine car?"

A black Cadillac is coming toward us, going way too fast. Without slowing down much, it swerves off the road and drives across the school-yard, right through the circle of stones where Miss Holmes put seeds out for her new garden. Laying hard on the brakes, the Cadillac stops under the sycamore tree.

Me and my teammates empty the field and huddle together. "Who do we know with a Cadillac?" asks Mason.

"Nobody!" we say all together.

The back doors of the Cadillac open.

Isaac gets out on one side, and Philly Dan gets out on the other. Each one's got a wide grin on his face.

"Hey, fellas!" yells Philly Dan. "We've got company."

"And you'll never guess who," says Isaac.

Right then, the front door of the car opens and the tallest, thinnest fellow I've ever seen unfolds himself from the driver's seat and walks toward us.

"No need to guess, boys. I am the one and only Satchel Paige, the best pitcher in baseball," he says, smiling wide to show his gold tooth.

"Oh my lordy! Satchel Paige?" I yell.

Satchel Paige is Sunday-dressed-up in a dark gray suit, white shirt, red tie, and a straw hat with a gray band. All I can do is stare with my mouth open as he comes closer and closer, my heart beating louder with his every step.

"Criss-a-mighty! Is that really him?" asks Mason.

I can't talk. I can hardly breathe. My favorite pitcher, my hero, is right here at Walker Field. Is this really happening?

Now a second man gets out of the front seat of the car. He's dressed in a dark blue jacket, light blue shirt, dark pants, and a Kansas City Monarchs baseball cap. "Well, he might be great, but Satchel is never modest," he says, laughing.

"So, which one of you is Li'l Moses?" asks Satchel. His eyes fall on each one of us.

"Gotta be this one, Satch," the second man says, pointing at me.

"Bless my soul," says Satchel. "Don't see how I missed it. Son, you look just like Mo. Isaac says you're starting to pitch like him too."

I open my mouth, but nothing comes out. Then I take in a deep breath. "Yes suh," I say.

"Fellas, this here is Mr. Satchel Paige, pitcher for the Kansas City Monarchs," says Isaac. Satchel takes off his hat and nods.

"And this brave soul, who dared to ride with Satchel all the way from Kansas City, is Mr. Buck O'Neil, second baseman for the Monarchs," says Philly Dan. Mr. O'Neil takes off his baseball cap and waves it in the air, a big smile on his face.

"Welcome, gentlemen. This is Walker Field, home of the Pender County Rangers," says Isaac. The Rangers all wave and grin, a dazed look on their faces.

"Nice ball field you've got out here in the country," says Satchel. "All you need is some bleachers and some real bases 'stead of them rocks set in the ground. Maybe I can help out with that, Isaac."

Mr. Buck O'Neil takes off his cap and scratches his head. "Well, that weren't no compliment, Satchel. But we don't need a fancy ball field to do what we do. Let's play some baseball."

Eyes wide, smiles on their faces, Rangers throw their hands up in the air and yell, "Yeah!!!"

"I've got to get comfortable first," says Mr. Satchel. He strolls back to the Cadillac, pulls off his jacket, hat, and tie, and throws each one of them onto the front seat. Then he walks back to the mound where the Rangers are standing.

He looks right at me. "'Fore we get the team on the field, I want to see Li'l Mo here pitch a few balls."

My heart stops. Sweat pops out on my forehead. A wave of heat goes all through me.

"Yes suh," I say, but I don't move.

Mr. Buck walks over and grabs my arm. "Come on, son. Satchel may look like a hound dog, but he won't bite."

"Don't be bad-mouthin' me in front of these boys, Buck."

"That was a compliment, Satch." Mr. Buck laughs.

Most of the team scatters to the edge of the field to watch. Mr. Satchel, Mr. Buck, Isaac, and Philly Dan join them.

I step onto the mound. Mason is behind the plate. A few of the Rangers line up to bat. I tip my cap to Mason. We're all set. I close my eyes for a moment and think about Daddy Mo. Wonder how he felt when he was getting ready to pitch and Mr. Satchel was watching. He'd be so proud if he could see me. Now I wish I had his baseball cap and the glove he left to Isaac to bring me luck. Then all a sudden, I feel a spirit beside me, warming me through and through. *Hello, Daddy Mo.*

I open my eyes, take in a deep breath, wind up, and throw my best fastball over home plate. It lands in Mason's glove in spite of Smokey Joe's mighty swing. For my second pitch, I remember my new windup and raise my left leg high in the air before letting the fastball go. It flies into Mason's glove and I don't think that Smokey Joe even saw it. Strike two. Proud of myself, but a little nervous, I forget to raise my leg on the third fastball and Smokey Joe knocks it deep into the outfield, right into Raymond D.'s glove.

Hank is next at bat. I lean forward and squint as I see Mason sign, telling me to throw a slider. We both know that I need to bring my best stuff or Hank will make me look like a rookie. I also need the courage to switch between my fastball and a slider if I want to strike him out.

I can feel Daddy Mo's spirit with me. With a fastball and two sliders, Hank's turn at bat is a strikeout. He smiles as he walks away, something I've never seen before.

Isaac and Philly Dan, Mr. Satchel and Mr. Buck stroll out to the mound. The Rangers gather 'round too. Mr. Buck hits me on the back, hard. "Man! That was some good pitching, son."

"Pretty good for a young pup," says Satchel. "Time for you to learn something from the master."

My mouth drops open. "Are you gonna teach me how to throw your hesitation pitch, Mr. Satchel?"

He throws his head way back and laughs. "No, son. That's my secret. It's what makes me special. I'm going to teach *you* how to throw a curveball."

I go hot and cold all over. Me! Taught by Mr. Satchel Paige!

Mason runs to take his place behind home plate.

"Give me that ball, son. When you add the curveball to what you can do now, won't be a batter in these parts can touch you." Mr. Satchel wraps his huge hands around the ball, placing his fingers near the seams same as for a slider. "See here?" he says.

I cover my mouth and laugh under my breath. It would take ten years of growing for my hand to be big enough to wrap around the baseball like his hand does.

"Now you try it."

"Yes suh." I wrap my fingers around another baseball, just like he showed me.

"Good. Now watch the way my wrist snaps when I let go of the ball."

Mr. Satchel winds up and I can't believe what I'm seeing. He leans way back, so far, seems like he'll fall onto the ground. Then, in a move that is so fast that none of us see it, he throws a curveball straight into Mason's glove. We all stare at him with our mouths open, amazed by the way that his body moves.

Mr. Buck laughs. "Lots of folks have to stare for a minute or two when they see Satch lean back like that. But he never falls, I promise you."

"Um, Mr. Satchel? Could you do that again, please?" I ask politely.

"All right," he says. "Keep your eye on the ball this time, sonny."

"Yes suh."

Mr. Satchel throws four more curveballs, each one sailing through the air, then dropping down just as it crosses home plate and landing in Mason's glove. Darned if I saw a single one of them leave his hand. Then he gives me the ball. I take in a deep breath, wind up, and throw six curveballs into the dirt and four into Mason's glove.

"Pretty good, son," says Mr. Satchel. "Now give me ten more. Throw harder this time."

I do what I'm told, but I'm too scared to use my new windup. What would "the master" think if he saw it again?

"That was great," says Mr. Buck after I throw the last one. "Hey, Satch, we might as well give the team some hitting and fielding tips while we're here."

"Yeah!" the Rangers yell.

For the next hour or so, Mr. Satchel, Mr. Buck, Isaac, and Philly Dan wander around the field working with first one Ranger and then another, helping him to play his position better. Then Mr. Satchel walks over to the trunk of his car, opens it, and pulls out a quart jar of lemonade. He turns it up to his mouth and guzzles it down.

Mr. Buck shakes his head. "Well, Satch is done with baseball for today. We'd better be getting on the road."

Sure enough, Mr. Satchel waves his hand in the air. Mr. Buck goes over and the rest of us follow.

"Time to go, Buck. We need to be in Richmond before sundown," he explains.

"Man, we'd have to fly to do that, Satch," says Mr. Buck. "You boys had better pray that I get to Richmond in one piece," he adds, laughing.

"Oh shush. You know you love riding with me, Buck."

Mr. Satchel reaches into the open window of the car, pulls out his suit coat and hat, and puts them back on. He grabs his tie and, without looking, makes a perfect knot. Then he shoves his long legs into the car and starts the engine.

Oh no! This can't be over. My head spins, and my throat feels tight.

"Mr. Satchel?" I say, running over to the Cadillac. "I sure would like to come to Kansas City and see you pitch a game sometime."

"That will be fine, son. Whenever Isaac and Philly Dan go back, you can come with them."

Isaac walks up to us. "Um, school's not out yet, Satch, and Papa Vee's got something special for Cato to do this summer. Maybe next year."

"That would be great. Buck! Let's hit the road."

Before Mr. Buck can walk around to the rider's side, Mr. Satchel is already pulling off.

"You planning to leave me?" yells Mr. Buck, laughing.

Mr. Satchel stops the car, but as soon as Mr. Buck gets in, he screeches across the schoolyard, before the door is even closed.

"See ya, fellas. It was fun!" yells Mr. Buck.

The Cadillac lurches onto the road and soon disappears into the distance. The Rangers stare in silence 'til they're out of sight. No one sees my eyes glisten with tears.

That was the best day of my whole life.

# Chapter 28

## THE PENDER COUNTY-NEW HANOVER GAMES

—

Today the Rangers play our second game against the New Hanover Marlins. And everything—I mean *everything*—is different this time.

I feel it as soon as the Rangers start on our way to Poplar Field, running past folks headed to the ball game. The air is thick with excitement, not fear. The Marlins must have told their friends and families that the Pender County–New Hanover Games were gonna be worth it. There's lots of people out: laughing, talking, and carrying picnic baskets full of food. The smell of it makes my mouth water! Women and girls are here, too, gloriously dressed up in their Sunday best. Equal numbers of white and colored have come, and though they aren't mingling with one another, they're sharing the road just fine.

Papa Vee, Rev, Mr. Harlee Jamison, Harlee Junior, and the boys from the Tidewater Colored League teams are here, too. Hope and her friends are sitting amongst them, and Mr. D. K. Johnson and his building crew sit right behind them.

The Rebel Clan has claimed the same spot they had before, right behind third base, which bothers me, but I try not to think about it.

The umpire flips a coin to start the game. The Rangers choose heads, and this time the toss is in our favor.

"Home team," I say. That means Marlins are first at bat.

As soon as I step onto the mound, I see Trace looking my way. He holds me in a determined stare. We both know what this game is about.

It's a matchup between a white and a colored team—but it's also a battle between the two of us.

Mr. Luke and Daddy Mo didn't play the same position, and they never faced each other on the field. But me and Trace have that chance, and it will be a contest to see who's best.

The first batter is the same fella that always leads the Marlins lineup. Whenever he faces me, he strikes out on three pitches. And that's what happens now. Three fastballs. Three strikes for the first out. Mason looks at me and shakes his head.

Trace walks into the batter's box next. He seems confident, like a fella who's hit a few home runs. Mason sends a sign telling me to throw a slider. I nod and raise my glove up to my face, baseball tucked in my right hand. Knowing that Trace wouldn't be bothered by a threatening glare, I decide to use my new windup and simply send him my best pitch.

I take in a deep breath, raise my left leg high in the air, lean back slightly, and hurl the baseball as hard as I can. Trace swings, but the ball lands in Mason's glove.

"Strike one," the umpire yells.

I get into position, glove raised up to my chin, and wait for Trace to get ready. Mason sends the sign for another slider. I agree. This time, I concentrate even more on my windup, raising my leg higher than before and throwing the ball harder this time.

Trace swings. The ball catches the tip of the bat and lands in foul territory for strike two.

I can see the disappointment on Trace's face. He gets into batting position again. Mason signals to pitch another slider. I don't agree. Trace is a smart fella. He got a piece of that last pitch and if I throw him another slider, he'll knock that ball into kingdom come.

I decide to throw a fastball. I use my new windup to give it more speed and I throw it straight across the strike zone.

There's no mistaking the *whack* that we hear when Trace hits the ball. It rises up over the trees and out of sight. Trace jogs around the bases to celebrate.

Marlins fans cheer loudly. Their team scored a home run in the first inning! The boys in the Rebel Clan have left their seats and are dancing on the edge of the ball field, like the Marlins have already won the game.

I glance at my cheering squad—Papa Vee, Rev, Mr. Harlee Jamison, Harlee Junior, Hope and her friends, Mr. D. K. Johnson and his crew, and the boys from the Tidewater Colored League teams. They all look pretty calm. It's just the first inning.

Freight Train is the next batter. He walks up slow and easy, a Cheshire-cat grin on his face. I can feel the back of my neck tingle.

Before stepping into the batter's box, he looks to his left at the fellas in red, then leans forward, squats a bit so that his legs are bowed, and scratches himself under his armpits. The boys in the Rebel Clan hoot like monkeys. Lordy. I turn my back on the lot of them and face second base. In a moment, I turn back. Freight Train grins, steps into the batter's box, and raises his bat into position. A bitter taste comes into my mouth. I hold the ball and glove up to my face, stare at Freight Train for as long as I dare, then wind up and aim my fastball at Mason's glove.

Freight Train swings hard. And misses.

"Strike one!" the umpire yells.

Freight Train rolls his eyes and raises his bat into position again. I wind up and throw a fastball even harder than the one before. Then my forehead wrinkles, and my eyes narrow. Is Freight Train leaning in, ever so slightly? The ball bounces off of his shoulder.

"Ow!" he yells. He rubs his shoulder, scrunches his face up like he's in pain, then trots off to first base. When he gets there, he stares at me, a wide, evil grin on his face.

I look at Mason. We both shake our heads, knowing that he stepped into the ball and got hit on purpose. The umpire doesn't even call it.

By now I know that the fourth Marlins batter, a short, squat fella, hits like the first batter in the lineup. Without thinking much about it, I throw him a fastball. He swings. Strike. Another fastball. Another Swing. Strike! On the third pitch, he hits a grounder to center field and the ball rolls right through Raymond D.'s hands. The runner is safe at first. Then our shortstop, Skeeter, runs over to capture the ball and throws it to me, lightning fast.

No need to think. I throw to Mason because I know that when the last batter hit, Freight Train started running for home, aiming to score. He slides into home plate, the toe of his shoe touching the bag right after Mason tags him. For a moment, it's so quiet, seems like everybody's stopped breathing.

The umpire calls, "You're out!"

Silence.

Then the yelling starts.

Everybody is standing up, their mouths open, hands waving in the air. The Rangers fans are cheering. The Marlins fans are booing. At home plate, Freight Train is shouting, his purple face inches from the umpire's, spit flying.

With a nod from Mr. Luke, three Marlins players grab Freight Train and pull him off the field.

Two outs. One man on base.

By the time the fifth Marlins batter steps into the batter's box, the frown on Mason's face says *Get out of this inning!* From game one, we know that this fella is one of their best hitters.

Throw a curveball, Mason signals. Sweat pops out on my forehead. *Can I do that? Can I throw a pitch that Mr. Satchel taught me just the other day?*

Mason must see the doubt in my eyes. He gives me a thumbs-up.

I glance to my right and see the Rangers cheering squad showing a whole row of thumbs turned up. Standing at the edge of the field, Isaac and Philly Dan turn their thumbs up too.

Heaven help this batter.

I take in a deep breath, bring my glove up to my face, and think about the blood that flows through my veins.

If I want to strike this fella out with my curveball, Daddy Mo will help.

I raise my left leg high in the air, lean back slightly, then lunge forward and release the ball just like Satchel showed me. It hurls toward home plate, then drops slightly just before it lands perfectly in Mason's glove. The batter swings hard, but too late. And...

"Strike!"

The batter looks confused, but he raises his bat again right away. I pitch another curveball that lands in Mason's glove with a *thunk*.

"Strike!" the umpire calls.

This time, the batter drops his bat for a moment and looks back at Mason. Then he looks toward his teammates. Freight Train starts to walk onto the field, but Mr. Luke holds him back. The evil look on his face is the same as when we played shadow ball.

Though he doesn't need to, Mason signals for me to throw another curveball, and that's what I do. The batter swings. And misses again.

"Strike!" the umpire calls.

Side out! At last! The first inning is over and the Marlins scored only one run!

The Rangers are not so lucky. For our turn at bat, Trace strikes out every single batter at the bottom of the first. The Rangers don't score a single run. Me and Mason look at one another and shake our heads. This is no way to start a ball game!

But the ending is a different story.

The battle between the Rangers and the Marlins in this first game of the Pender County–New Hanover Games ends with a difference of only one run in the final score.

The teams are evenly matched in fielding and hitting. It's home runs by Hank and Smokey Joe in the fifth and Hank's home run in the ninth that give the Rangers the winning edge.

Me and Trace are evenly matched as pitchers too. We both strike out most players who come to bat, and strike out all of them in the sixth and eighth innings. I'm betting we'll need to play all five games before the winner of the Pender County–New Hanover Games is declared.

| | 1st | 2nd | 3rd | 4th | 5th | 6th | 7th | 8th | 9th | | Runs | Hits | Errors |
|---|---|---|---|---|---|---|---|---|---|---|---|---|---|
| Marlins | 1 | 1 | 1 | 1 | 0 | 0 | 1 | 0 | 1 | | 6 | 12 | 3 |
| Rangers | 0 | 1 | 1 | 1 | 2 | 0 | 1 | 0 | 1 | | 7 | 14 | 2 |

I almost forgot about the Rebel Clan. After every inning, Sheriff Pridgeon and two of his deputies got up from their seats and marched in front of the bleachers. Freight Train's eyes always followed them. The boys in red did too—there were no bone-chilling rebel yells or dogs let loose on the field. When the final play is made and the Rangers win the game, we hear low growling from them. The sound rises in their throats until they're all barking like dogs again. I look around quickly to see if there are any real dogs nearby. Sheriff Pridgeon and his deputies march in front of the bleachers, a little faster this time, and stare into the crowd. The boys in red are drawing attention to themselves, but they're not doing anything dangerous or against the law. What they do next, though, I would call heart-stopping. They all turn their gaze directly on me. Then they ball their right hands into tight fists and pound them into their open palms. Me and Mason look at one another. What now? The Rebel Clan then marches off Poplar Field double time, yelling, "Hut! Hut! Hut! Hut!" as they go and walking so close to the sheriff and his deputies that they almost touch. We all stare at them until they're out of sight.

Players and fans trickle off the ball field and head for home on foot or in their pickup trucks. The chatter is loud again, normal, and there's plenty of laughing. Seems like folks enjoyed themselves. And no one can say that the Rangers and the Marlins didn't play hard.

"Well, that was a hoot!" says Mr. Luke as me and Mason and Trace gather outside the ball field.

Trace looks at me sideways. "We're gonna beat the tar out of you next game."

"We're gonna practice so hard you won't be able to do that," says Mason, laughing.

"Ain't nothin' gonna help you next game," says Trace, grinning.

I shake my head. With three or four more chances to play, nobody knows who will win the Pender County–New Hanover Games.

"Well, I'm satisfied." Mr. Luke grins. "You boys are going to be baseball buddies for sure."

Me and Trace roll our eyes.

"Hey!" yells Mr. Luke, pointing toward the sky. "That's an awful lot of smoke over there. Must be a fire. What's in that direction?"

"Walker Field!" I say.

"And our schoolhouse!" cries Mason.

"Well, I'd sure say something's burning!" Mr. Luke gets into his truck.

"Where're you going, Daddy?" asks Trace.

"To find Rev and Vernon. We'll get a work crew, some barrels of water, and put out the fire if there is one. You boys get on the back of the truck."

I shake my head as I rush away from him. "I need to see what's happening, Mr. Luke—need to get over to the school in a hurry!"

"Let's go, Cato!" Mason runs toward the path that we both know to be a shortcut through the woods.

I follow him, yelling over my shoulder, "If there's a fire, we have to save Miss Holmes's books!"

"Hey! I'm going too!" Trace dashes after me.

"Boys! Don't put yourselves in danger!" Mr. Luke jumps out of the truck and cups his hands around his mouth. "Smoke can kill you just as good as flames!"

# Chapter 29
## SAVING LANGSTON HUGHES

Though the schoolhouse is more'n a mile away, we can smell the smoke when we're halfway there. We're running at an even pace, single file, to stay on the narrow deer path through the woods.

"Hey! What're we even gonna do when we get there?" puffs Mason.

"Blankets from the closet! Water from the well!" I yell.

"Where's the well?" asks Trace.

"Out back!" calls Mason.

We come out of the woods at a bend in the road just below Walker Field. From where we are, the schoolhouse is on the other side of the clearing.

Two things set my heart to pounding.

First, there's smoke rising over the roof of the schoolhouse, though I don't see flames.

Second, the green pickup truck sitting in front of the schoolhouse, its doors wide open, looks a lot like the truck that someone leaned out of to shoot at me and Philly Dan.

The skin on the back of my neck tingles. "Mason, go to the back of the school," I say, sounding calmer than I feel. "Me and Trace will see what's happening on the other side of the building."

The three of us start to run across the clearing, but stop after only a few steps. Two white boys are milling around the schoolhouse, one back near the well, one on the front porch.

They're both wearing red.

"I don't believe it!" gasps Trace. "They're trying to be Red Shirts! Your grandpa was right!"

"We all know these boys. It's Digger and Mouse—just like at the church."

They've both got tin cans in their hands. Kerosene. Mouse is pouring it around the well, and Digger's pouring it on the porch.

"Trying to set a fire again," I say grimly.

"Not today!" Mason balls his fists. "Wish I had a shotgun now!"

"No, Mason," says Trace. "We'll have to use the weapons the good Lord gave us."

Me and Mason look at him, surprised. Then, before I can really even catch my breath, I see Freight Train step out from the other side of the schoolhouse carrying a can in one hand. He's changed from his Marlins uniform. Now he's wearing a red T- shirt like his cousins and a red kerchief around his neck.

I always figured he was one of them. Now I know.

Right then, Freight Train sees the three of us. He reaches into his pocket, pulls something out, and says something to Digger. The two of them strike matches and toss them onto the porch. Yellow- and orange-colored flames spread so fast that Digger has to jump to the ground to escape.

Still watching us, Freight Train gives the tin can he's holding to Mouse, who goes to shake kerosene onto the back steps.

"I'm gonna beat the livin' tar out of that rat!" Mason takes off running.

Flames are rising from the porch, black smoke is rising from the back. Their work done, Digger and Freight Train hurry toward the pickup truck.

"Freight Train's mine," I say.

"I'll take Digger," says Trace.

We both race across the clearing, aiming to tackle these rats before they get away. We make it. Trace grabs Digger's shirt and throws him to the ground. But Freight Train sees me coming, whirls around, and rushes toward me.

We've both been hankering for this fight since we first met.

Arms out, head down like a bull charging, he's aiming to butt me in the chest. But I've learned a thing or two from tussling with the Rangers and with Isaac. When Freight Train is so close I can almost feel the heat of his body, I tuck my head down and roll onto the ground, ducking under his outstretched arm. In a moment, I'm back on my feet.

He turns and rushes at me again, then leaps into the air and crashes down on top of me. I fall backward onto the ground. Freight Train folds his arms across my chest and presses down hard.

I can't breathe! His face is inches away from mine, and his breath is hot and sour. Dark eyes burn with hatred.

"You a trouble-making neega. Don't ever know yo' place."

With each word, Freight Train presses harder on my chest. Feels like he'll break my ribs. My head spins. Lordy!

*Am I going to die today? Is this how Daddy Mo felt at the end?*

For a moment, my mind goes blank. And then, just when I'm sure that I'll never see Papa Vee, Gran, Hope, Rev, or Isaac again, the pain stops.

Freight Train rolls off of me and pushes himself up off the ground. For a moment, he just stands there, hands in his pockets, staring at me.

"You know, that don't feel nearly as good as I thought it would. Not worth it, anyhow."

I stare back.

He turns and walks in the direction of the truck. "Digger! You and Mouse better win them fights pretty quick or I'm gonna leave the both of you!"

Trace and Digger are at the back of the truck, wallowing on the ground. Can't figure who's winning. Then Mason reappears. "You need some help, Trace? Mouse ran off on me!"

Freight Train starts the engine of the truck, and Digger's eyes get big. He hits Trace hard in the face with his fist, then scrambles up, climbs in the passenger side, and slams the door shut. Freight Train guns the engine one last time and drives off, veering from side to side.

As they speed away from the schoolhouse, Freight Train hangs his head out the window and yells, "Bye, suckahs!"

The fire on the porch is raging. The crackle of the flames and the bitter smells of kerosene and burnt wood fill the air.

Mason helps Trace get to his feet. "What're we gonna do now?" he cries. "Fire's too big for us to put out."

"We wait for the grown folks to get here," says Trace. "Like Daddy said."

"No!" I yell. "I've got to save Miss Holmes's books!" I'm standing in front of the schoolhouse, but I see no way in.

"Remember what Daddy said about smoke, Cato!"

Ignoring Trace, I start for the back of the schoolhouse.

Mason throws up his hands. "You can't tell him nothin'. Come on, Trace!"

Black smoke from the fire on the other side of the schoolhouse is curling up through the steps, but the back door is clear of flames. So I run up the steps, open the door, and go inside. Heat slams into me so fierce that my skin hurts. I ought to go back to safety, but I don't. The rush of air from the open door causes the flames inside to shoot up and burn brighter. But that's not my biggest problem. Mr. Luke was right. The smoke stings my eyes. It burns my nose. I can hardly breathe. I pull a kerchief out of my pocket and cover my nose. It doesn't help.

Mason and Trace have the good sense to stop at the door. Trace leaves a small crack and the two of them stand and watch.

Mason yells at me, "Cato, whatever you're doing, hurry up, man!"

The bookshelf is near the back door, thank goodness. I've seen Miss Holmes grab a book to read aloud to the class a hundred times. Can't stop to see which ones are her favorites or where her precious Langston Hughes books are. I just grab an armful of them.

Trace opens the door wider and takes a step inside. "There's flames in here, Cato. You need to come out. Now!"

"Take these! I want to get just a few more." I run, shove the books into Trace's arms, and turn to rush back to the bookcase. I hear Mason say, "What? He's not coming out yet?"

The smoke is thicker now. Flames from the front porch are feeding the flames inside. I grab another armful of books and rush toward the back door. Mason holds it open, and I dash outside. The three of us run across the schoolyard and across the clearing 'til we get to Walker Field, our arms full of books. We drop them on the ground, slump down under the sycamore tree, and watch the fire burn.

I'm wrung-out from sucking in smoke. My spirit is crushed 'cause we couldn't put out the fire, couldn't stop Freight Train and his cousins from starting it.

Pretty soon we see a convoy of ten pickup trucks driving toward the schoolhouse, Rev and Mr. Luke out front. Each one is carrying barrels full of water on the back. Grown folks coming to save the day. Too late.

Again.

# Chapter 30
## A THIMBLEFUL OF JUSTICE

It's been a day since the fire, and I'm kind of lost. Thought I was a hero when me and Mason stopped the Rebel Clan from burning down Saint John's Church. But now I feel like a wad of bubble gum on the bottom of somebody's shoe. The three of us, me and Mason and Trace, couldn't do a thing to stop Freight Train and his cousins.

Reckon I'm not a hero after all.

It's a hot afternoon. Papa Vee sits down beside me on the front porch steps. I've got a knife in one hand and a piece of wood in the other. Call myself whittlin'.

"You're moving too fast, son. That wood will be a sliver in just a little while."

"Got plenty of wood next to me, Papa Vee."

"That's not the point. Whittlin's got a purpose. Clears your head, helps you think on hard things, figure them out. Won't happen if you move your knife like that."

I stop cutting strips off the piece of wood I'm holding and turn to look at him.

"Calms the mind too," he says. "Why do you think I do it all the time?"

I shrug.

Papa Vee takes his knife out of his pocket and folds out the blade. "Give me a piece." I do, then watch as he shaves the wood in slow, easy strokes. "See how I move this knife?"

I throw away the piece of wood I've ruined and start on another, moving the knife slow and easy just like Papa Vee.

"So...how you feel about the fire and all?" he asks.

"I don't know, Papa Vee. This summer's messed up. Since we got all mixed up with the Marlins, seems like nothing's gone right."

"Well, it has been exciting, I'll give you that. But you're becoming a fine pitcher—'specially with that new windup of yours."

"You like my windup?"

"Like it? Don't matter who likes it or don't like it. You get the job done. The Rangers beat the Marlins, didn't they?"

"We did!" I smile. "But even with baseball...not everything's good. I won't be going to Kansas City this year. You don't trust me enough for that."

"Boy, are you whining? Isaac hasn't been well enough to go, with or without you."

I hesitate. "Even if he was, you don't trust me, don't think . ]I can be useful to Isaac."

Papa Vee stops whittlin', lays his knife down, and looks at me. "Fair enough, son. The things you've done this summer show me that you are well on your way to being a man."

*What?* My mouth drops open, so I turn away from Papa Vee. I don't even look at him when a big ole grin spreads all across my face. No, I just keep whittlin', slow and easy.

Isaac and Philly Dan come out onto the porch.

"What're our star pitcher and his grandpa up to?" asks Isaac.

*Star pitcher?* Now I *have* to stop whittlin'. I lay down the knife and raise my hand to my mouth to hide an even wider grin.

Isaac leans over, trying to see my face. "Are you two having a whittlin' fest?"

"Oh no!" yells Philly Dan. "This is so Southern! No disrespect, Papa Vee."

Isaac rolls his eyes. "We are in Carolina, Philly."

"Country boy!" teases Philly Dan.

"You ought to try it. Calms me right down when I'm mad as..." Isaac glances at Papa Vee.

"Well, look-a-here, Cato," says Papa Vee. "Your boy Mason's coming."

"Man, he's running full-out," says Isaac.

Papa Vee laughs. "Looks like he's got his shorts in a wad again."

"Sheriff Pridgeon! Comin' this way!" cries Mason, skidding to a stop in front of us.

By now the sheriff has caught up with him. He slows his pickup truck and stops right beside the porch.

"I'm looking for Vernon," he says, leaning out of the window.

"He's here." I point.

A white man visitin' brings everybody out. Gran and Hope are standing on the front porch now.

"Morning, Vernon," says Sheriff Pridgeon, getting out.

"Morning, Sheriff," says Papa Vee.

The sheriff tips his hat in Gran's direction. "Morning, Nina. Daddy sends his r'gards, says he loved that apple pie you sent him last week. Wouldn't mind having another one."

"Just baked one this morning," says Gran, smiling. "You can take it to him." Gran goes inside and comes back out with a pie wrapped in a tea towel.

"Thank you, Nina. This will brighten Daddy's day." Sheriff Pridgeon nods. "He's ailing, but he's doing good for near eighty."

The sheriff sets the pie on the hood of his truck. Then his mood changes, and the corners of his mouth turn down.

"Luke Blackburn's been to see me three or four times these past weeks. There's been plenty of trouble on account of these baseball games the boys've been playing. Don't know why..."

The sheriff looks at Mason and me. He rubs his chin.

"Now, Luke told me about your schoolhouse being set afire. Saw for myself that it's burnt to the ground."

"Yep," says Papa Vee, narrowing his eyes.

The Sheriff looks away. He scratches his neck, takes off his cap, and puts it back on again. "I know it might seem like we don't do nothing when you people got trouble, but I do the best I can. You know how things are, Vernon."

The sheriff looks right at Papa Vee, but Papa Vee looks away.

There's a short silence. Sheriff Pridgeon takes a pipe out of his pocket, taps it against the palm of his hand to shake the stale tobacco free, and sticks it into his mouth. He doesn't light it, though.

"Anyhow," he continues, "this is different. I reckon we can do something about this fire.

"Luke said that his boy, Trace, saw the fellas that started it—told me that him and your boy here even fought with 'em and tried to save the school, but the fire was too hot to put out. Is that right?"

Sheriff Pridgeon gazes in my direction. I feel a rush of heat all over. My heart starts beating faster.

"Yes suh." I wipe sweat from my forehead with my palm. If I'm going to name them, it has to be now. "Me and Trace and Mason here saw Freight Train and his cousins, Digger and Mouse, pour kerosene on the schoolhouse and set it on fire."

Sheriff Pridgeon nods and turns back to Papa Vee. "Here's what's going to happen, Vernon.

"We're pretty sure that Freight Train and his cousin, Digger, are the ringleaders for the Carolina boys who're trying to be Red Shirts." He shifts the cold pipe he's holding from one hand to the other. "They're acting just like their kinfolk; Digger's great-grandpa in South Carolina and Freight Train's great-uncle in Wilmington, they were both part of the Red Shirts, long ago. Sheriff Loney even tells me they've got plenty of boys in red T-shirts making trouble in Charleston.

"So we're going to send Digger and the other one, Mouse, right back to South Carolina. It's where they're from, anyhow, and it's time they go back. I'll lock 'em up if I see 'em in New Hanover County again."

He glances over the faces looking back at him.

"But Freight Train is a New Hanover boy, and we can take care of our own. I'll make him clean the jailhouse and run errands for me every day for six months or so. Luke tells me he's off the baseball team, too. All that ought to get him to thinking about what he done."

Papa Vee raises his hand to his face and scratches his chin. His eyes narrow even more. "That all?" he says finally. "Well. Thank you kindly for telling us, Sheriff Pridgeon."

"Now, Vernon, you know how things are around here. I couldn't do a thing about any of this 'fore I had the right witness—'fore Luke's boy would say what he saw."

So my word alone wasn't worth a thing. Why'd he even ask me who the boys were?

Then, with nary a nod or a goodbye, Sheriff Pridgeon turns and walks to his pickup truck, grabs the apple pie off the hood, and gets in. He sets the pie on the seat beside him, starts the engine, and drives off.

Everyone is silent for a while. Then Isaac shakes his head. "Well now, did you hear what the sheriff said? He wasn't waiting for the *right* witness—he was waiting for a *white* witness."

Me and Philly Dan both look at Isaac, wide-eyed. Didn't expect him to say that out loud.

"Don't let it trouble you, son," says Papa Vee. "This is how things are for a colored man. Truth is, a thimbleful of justice is better than none at all."

"Oh boy," says Isaac, sitting down on the porch step. "Got my knife. Gimme one of those pieces of wood, Cato." With that, he starts cutting shards off the stick as fast as he can, just like Papa Vee told me not to.

Philly Dan takes a knife out of his pocket, unfolds the blade, and sits down next to Isaac. "I'll take one of those sticks, li'l brother."

I hand the last stick to Philly Dan, then get up to forage through the yard to find another one for me. The way I'm thinking, it's got to be a whole lot bigger so it can last a while.

# Chapter 31
## OUT OF THE ASHES

When Miss Holmes heard that Pender County Normal School had been burned to the ground, she fainted and would've hit the floor if Rev hadn't caught her. Gran brought her to our house, put her to bed, and gave her a hot toddy to make her sleep.

"Her heart's just broke to pieces," Gran had said sadly.

Most all of the colored folks in Pender County felt the same. It was like a favorite aunt or cousin died and we were having a wake for them: there were visitors at our house day and night after the fire. They sat on the porch and stood in the yard, swapping stories about when they, or their sons and daughters, went to Pender County Normal School.

Three days after the fire, folks started drifting down to where the schoolhouse was, bringing pieces of lumber and tools and leaving them there overnight. Work crews started showing up in the evenings and all day on Saturdays. Now there's somebody there all the time, working on the schoolhouse.

Mr. D. K. Johnson from our own Saint John's Church is foreman. He puts everybody who wants to work into a work crew with a boss man to help them follow orders. I'm the boss man for the Rangers work crew. We mostly haul things around in wheelbarrows and hand nails, tools, and such to the workers. But we have fun too, punching one another and fooling around. Every now and again, boys from Tidewater Colored League teams stop by and join the Rangers work crew. One day, Trace even brought most all of the Marlins team by to help with the building—but he and Mr. Luke show up every day.

The new foundation of the schoolhouse was laid yesterday. This morning, Mr. Luke brought a crew of white men from New Hanover County to help so the schoolhouse can be rebuilt faster. With all of these workers, they'll prob'ly raise the walls into place by the end of the week.

Rev is standing under the sycamore tree where Gran is packing up leftovers from lunch from the back of Papa Vee's truck. He should be working with his own crew, but he's watching Mr. Luke and the other white men from New Hanover. I wander over to see what he's up to.

"Mercy. In all my days, I've never seen so many white folks come to help us out like this," he says.

Gran shakes her head. "They're here because of Luke, Amos. Maybe now you can let go of some of the venom you've had for him."

"I'm working on it, Mama J. Still working on it."

Rev may be stuck in how he feels about Mr. Luke, but I'm not. "Gran? I've been thinking."

"Well, hallelujah!" She laughs. "Sorry, Cato. After talking to Amos, I needed to laugh. What's on your mind?"

"Mr. Luke must be a good man."

"Oh! What makes you say that?"

"Well...he loved Daddy Mo and he still feels the pain of losing him, like us."

"Yes, son, he does." She squeezes my shoulder. "It's mighty grown-up of you to see something that Amos can't see."

"What if we invited Mr. Luke and Trace to Daddy Mo's birthday dinner? Would that be all right?"

"We? Sounds like you're the one who wants to invite them."

"Well, yes."

"Then go ahead." She motions her hand at me. "Don't think there's a soul in this family who would find any fault with that."

"You sure, Gran?"

"Maybe Amos...but he'll get over it."

"Did he ever like Mr. Luke, before Daddy Mo died?"

"No. Loathed the ground he walked on."

"How come?"

"Well, Daddy Mo and Luke spent pretty near every day together from the time they was four or five 'til Moses left for Kansas City. Amos come to live with us when he was seven and Moses was ten. By then, the older boys was thick as thieves. There was never any room for Amos."

"Oh," I say. Tells me a lot about Rev that I didn't know.

My eyes wander across the yard to where Mr. Luke is talking to some of the white men from New Hanover who've come to help today.

"I don't feel that way about Mr. Luke, Gran. So here I go. Today's as good as any to ask him to come to Daddy Mo's birthday dinner."

Gran kisses me on the forehead before I turn and walk toward Mr. Luke.

"Mr. Luke, could I have a word with you?" I ask.

"Why sure, Cato." We walk over to his pickup truck. "What's on your mind?"

"I want you to come to Daddy Mo's birthday dinner this year, like you used to. Trace is invited too."

Mr. Luke jerks his head around, stares at me for a moment, then quickly looks away. He takes in a breath so deep, I can hear it. "Have you talked to Amos about this? I don't know if he would want me to come."

"But things are different now, Mr. Luke. From what I can tell, you miss Daddy Mo as much as we do. That's what his birthday dinner is all about."

"Now are you sure you want to make Amos mad?"

"Rev's a preacher, Mr. Luke. Maybe now's the time for him to try to be understanding."

"Whoa! Now that would be a blessing."

"Well, are you coming?" I ask. "Are you and Trace coming?"

Mr. Luke nods, a wide grin spreading across his face. "Trace and I will be mighty proud to come to Mo's birthday dinner, Cato. When is it?"

"Um, I don't rightly know. Soon. Before Isaac goes back to Kansas City."

Mr. Luke sticks his hand out, and when we shake, he squeezes so hard it hurts.

"Thanks, Cato. This feels a lot like the forgiveness that I wanted," he says.

Mr. Luke rushes back to join the men from New Hanover and I go to find the Rangers work crew.

Around three o'clock I get thirsty and head for the water barrel. Rev comes up to me and touches my arm. I turn around to face him. He's frowning.

"What's the matter?" I ask.

"Just what were you and Luke Blackburn whispering about?"

"Oh." I lower my head and look at the ground.

"Spit it out, Cato. Your pondering just makes it harder to tell the truth."

"All right. I asked Mr. Luke and Trace to come to Daddy Mo's birthday dinner." I raise my head, look at Rev, then let out a long breath. He's not frowning anymore.

"Out of the mouths of babes...I can hear Mama J saying that now."

"I'm not a baby!" I yell.

"No, what I mean is that grown folks can learn a lot from young'uns, if they've got a mind to listen."

"What do you mean, Rev?"

"You inviting Luke to Mo's birthday dinner makes me think about forgiveness, Cato. All this time, I've been denying that losing Mo was painful for him too. Maybe it's time for me to act like a grown-up, to act like a preacher, and try to be decent to Luke."

Rev's words surprise me. "Then you don't mind if Mr. Luke comes?"

"No, Cato. I don't mind."

"One more thing, Rev. Mr. Luke said there was something he could've done different and Daddy Mo would've lived."

"Weren't nothing Luke could have done, Cato. 'Cept be on time, I reckon."

"If he'd picked up Daddy Mo soon as the bus let him off, Daddy Mo wouldn't have been there when the white boys came by."

"That's right. He wouldn't have been there. By being late, Luke never meant anything bad to happen. Papa Vee told you all about it, I guess."

"Gran told me."

"Oh." Rev raises an eyebrow, pats me on the back, and walks away.

I see him go over to Mr. D. K. Johnson and whisper in his ear. The two of them walk over to where Mr. Luke is standing with the men from New Hanover County. Then the three of them stroll away from the others and stand under the sycamore tree, talking with their heads tilting toward one another. I wish I could hear what they're saying; wish I knew what these newfound friends are up to.

# Chapter 32
## HOME-FIELD ADVANTAGE

School starts again on Monday. Miss Holmes will be overjoyed. But it's Saturday now and the Rangers are at Walker Field early, ready to practice. 'Fore we even get started, Rev and Mr. Luke drive up with two loads of secondhand boards on the backs of their pickup trucks. Trace is with them. Puzzled, we all stare. There's been a lot of building here the past two months. What are they up to now?

Rev gets out of his truck and walks over to us. "Walker Field looks kind of naked, fellas. You reckon it could use some bleachers?"

"Bleachers? Did you say bleachers?" I ask.

Rev nods and breaks out in a big grin.

I turn to my teammates. "Fellas, do we want bleachers?"

The Rangers cheer and holler, throwing their arms up in the air.

"We're winners and we deserve to have a better ball field!" shouts Raymond D.

"Criss-a-mighty! If we get bleachers, Walker Field will be better'n Poplar Field," says Mason.

"Hey now!" says Trace.

"All right, stop talking and get busy unloading this wood," says Rev.

"Thanks, Rev," I say, still reeling from the big surprise. "And thank you too, Mr. Luke."

"You're welcome, Cato." Mr. Luke takes his toolbox out of his truck. "The next time you boys want to see a professional-looking baseball field, you can look in your own backyard."

"I'm here to help," says Trace, grabbing one end of a board sliding off of Rev's truck.

"The more the merrier, Gran always says."

Mr. D. K. Johnson and some of the men who rebuilt the schoolhouse soon come by, ready to work. This time, the Rangers get to use hammers and nails a lot more than before. By late afternoon, the job is done. Walker Field now looks more like a baseball diamond on a picture postcard.

"D. K., what're we going to do with the rest of this wood?" asks Rev.

"Rev, didn't you tell us to build some—"

"Oh, just get busy, man!" says Rev, laughing.

The Rangers are puzzled again. What are the builders up to now? We watch as one group of men measures and saws planks of wood and puts them in a pile. The other group hammers away. In just a little while, we see a picnic table.

"Oh man!" yells Skeeter. "We've got a place to have a picnic now."

"Or a place to eat lunch when we're at school," says Raymond D., nodding in the direction of our new Elvira Holmes Normal School. Now Miss Holmes will walk under a sign with her name every day.

When three picnic tables are built, we put them under the sycamore tree, in the space between the schoolhouse and Walker Field. Now this small patch of dirt where Rangers spend most of our time feels even more like home. Rev gathers us all in a circle for a prayer of thanks. Then the other Rangers scatter on the field, ready for more practice, while the builders load up their tools and drive away.

I stand with my hands shoved deep into my pockets, thinking on the miracle of what happened here today. Trace walks up to me on his way to Mr. Luke's truck.

"Wow! This ball field looks great, Cato! You must feel pretty good right now."

"You have no idea," I say. "Now we've got a professional ball field too. You know what that means, don't you?"

"What?"

"Game two of the Pender County–New Hanover Games should be played here, at Walker Field."

"Sounds fair," says Trace, looking at me sideways. His face breaks out in a big grin. "Don't say anything 'til I have time to talk it over with the Marlins though."

"Deal."

The two of us step toward one another, hands outstretched, and seal the bargain with a powerful shake, as captains. And...

As friends.

# Chapter 33
## PROPHECY

Today we're celebrating Daddy Mo's birthday in a way that we never have before. The small family dinner that we've always had will now include Mr. Luke, Trace, Mason, and Philly Dan.

For me, this year started out to be the hardest since we lost Daddy Mo. Missing him and not knowing how he died made me so unhappy. Couldn't even go to Poplar Field by myself. Had to ask the Rangers to go with me. And that's how all the trouble started. But things have really turned around. Seems like this is going to be a very good year. I'm still hurting a lot 'cause Daddy Mo's not here, but I don't feel alone anymore. I know that Gran and Papa Vee, Rev, Hope, Isaac, and even Mr. Luke miss Daddy Mo just as much as me.

Hope comes outside and sits down beside me on the front porch steps.

"What's that in your hand?" I ask, lunging to snatch it from her.

Hope jumps off the step and onto the ground, raising the book high over her head. "Must be yours. There's a bunch of notes written in it and the last one says 'Dear Cato'."

"Thief! You been rummaging in my stuff, girl?"

"You left it in a chair in the kitchen. Tried to ignore it, but it kept calling, Read me! Read me!"

"So, what did you learn, Miss Nosey?"

Hope's face goes from playful to sad. She sits back down on the step beside me and holds the battered copy of *The Weary Blues* by Langston Hughes out in front of her. It's one of the books that I rescued from the fire.

"I cried when I read these notes."

"Didn't get any tears on my book, did you?"

Hope takes in a deep breath and ignores my teasing.

"I can hear Miss Holmes telling you what this is. A family heirloom, just like this locket I wear around my neck." Her hand wanders up to touch the locket that once belonged to our mother, Clarise. "I learned that this book was a family heirloom for Miss Holmes, then she gave it to Daddy Mo. When he died, Gran gave it back to Miss Holmes. And now she's giving it to you."

"Yep. It's hard to believe that Daddy Mo loved poetry. Nobody ever talks about that. Miss Holmes said that he even wrote poetry."

Hope's head snaps in my direction. "What? I wish we could have read something that he wrote."

She hands the book back to me. "After I cried, I read the notes over and over again; the one that Langston Hughes wrote to Miss Holmes, the one that Miss Holmes wrote to Daddy Mo, and the one that Miss Holmes wrote to you a few weeks ago. Finding out something new about Daddy Mo made me so happy inside."

"Yeah. Me too."

For a moment, me and Hope sit quietly. In my mind, I see Daddy Mo reading poems from *The Weary Blues*, see him write his own poems while sitting on the porch steps where we are right now. I glance at Hope and wonder if she's thinking about Daddy Mo too.

But Hope is staring at something in the distance. All a sudden, she stands, shading her eyes with one hand and pointing with the other. "We've got company. What in the world is that thing they're riding in?"

We see a strange-looking car coming toward us, looking like something out of a dream. It's bigger than Mr. Satchel's Cadillac and a lot longer. Can't figure what it's made out of. The hood and the top are shiny and gleam in the sun, but the side doors are dull. Looks like wood, the kind you see on a china closet in somebody's dining room.

The long car rolls into the front yard and stops under the sycamore tree. A face that I know and love leans out of the front window on the rider's side.

"Man! This is like riding on a cloud ." Rev grins as he opens the huge door, then stands with his chest puffed out, proudly staring at the car.

On the driver's side, Mr. Luke's head pops up as he gets out. "Is Vernon here?"

"I'll get Papa Vee," I say, going into the house.

Gran and Papa Vee are just coming out of the kitchen.

"What's all the racket?" asks Gran.

"Rev just rode up with Mr. Luke in the strangest looking car I've ever seen."

We all rush outside.

"Mornin', Luke," says Papa Vee.

"Morning, Vernon. Well, this is it. She's a beauty, don't you think?"

Papa Vee takes off his cap and scratches his head. "I didn't expect it to be this big, Luke. How many does it hold?"

Rev rushes over to Papa Vee, his arms waving in the air. "This baby can hold eight people easy, with plenty of room for somebody tall and big like me!"

The back doors of the car open. Trace gets out on one side and Mason gets out on the other. They both come over to where I'm standing.

"Hey," they say at the same time.

"Where'd Mr. Luke get such a strange-looking thing?" I ask.

Rev comes over and puts his arm on my shoulder. "Some folks call this a hackney wagon, Cato. I've seen a few in Wilmington at the train station, but this is my first time riding in one."

Rev is acting like a little boy with a Christmas toy. He even looks happy to be riding with Mr. Luke.

"Goodness, this car is so big!" yells Hope, sticking her head inside the open front window. "And it's got three rows of seats instead of two!"

I run over and stick my head into the back window to have a look for myself. Can't help but notice a cardboard box on the middle seat. When I pull my head out again, I see Papa Vee, Gran, Mr. Luke, and Rev staring at me, their hands covering their mouths, trying not to laugh.

"What's going on?" I ask, looking straight at Papa Vee.

"Nina?" says Papa Vee.

Gran reaches into her apron pocket, pulls out an envelope, and hands it to Papa Vee.

"I got a letter a few days ago, Cato. This will all make sense once you read it."

"Yes suh," I say, taking the letter from Papa Vee's hand. I look at the address in the corner and see who it's from. "Oh my lordy," I say.

"Who? Who's it from, Cato?" asks Hope. "Read it out loud. I want to hear."

I open the envelope, take the letter out, and read.

Dear Mr. Vernon Jones,

Thank you for the hospitality that you showed to Satchel Paige and me when we visited your home in North Carolina. Please tell Miss Nina that her ham biscuits were delicious. We ate them all the way to Richmond and enjoyed every bite.

I also want to thank you and Miss Nina for raising three wonderful sons. Isaac is an outstanding player for the Kansas City Monarchs and Cato is a mighty fine pitcher already. He not only looks like Moses, he pitches like him too. It is my hope that Cato will play for the Monarchs someday. And that is the reason for my letter, Mr. Jones. If Cato is to grow into the kind of pitcher that I know he can be, he must start his training now. At the very least, he must see professional baseball teams play in professional stadiums.

So, with your permission, sir, I would like to invite Cato to come and watch the Kansas City Monarchs play against the Homestead Grays in a five-game series in July. I will send tickets and pay for you to stay at the rooming house where Satchel and I stay sometimes.

Please let me know how many will be coming. Tell the Rangers I am sorry that I cannot invite the whole team. Also, I am hoping *that when all of you put your heads together, you can figure out a way to get here on your own.*

*Again, it was great meeting you and Miss Nina, Hope, and Rev. I look forward to seeing you and Cato in Kansas City in July.*

> *Sincerely,*
> *Mr. Buck O'Neil*
> *Second Baseman, the Kansas City Monarchs*

'Bout halfway through the letter, my heart starts pounding so loud, I can barely hear my own voice, but I keep reading 'til the end.

"Oh my lordy!" I say again, lowering the letter from my face.

"Surprise!" Gran walks over and gives me a big kiss on the cheek.

I blow out a long breath. My head spins. Don't know what I'm feeling right now. I'm overjoyed that Mr. Buck invited me to Kansas City and scared that Papa Vee will say no. But when I look at him, Papa Vee's got a big smile on his face, showing all of his teeth.

I can hardly get the words out. "Can I go, Papa Vee? Can I go to see the Monarchs play the Homestead Grays?"

Papa Vee is still grinning like I've never seen before. "Yep," he says simply.

I hold my breath, waiting for Papa Vee to say more. He doesn't. "How will I get there, Papa Vee?"

"Don't you see this bus we rode up in?" asks Rev, laughing.

"You'll be riding to Kansas City with Luke in this contraption," says Papa Vee.

"What?"

Mr. Luke nods his head. "My brother calls this a station wagon, Cato. He uses it to haul people and their satchels to and from the train station and the bus station. He's letting me borrow it in July so we can drive to Kansas City."

"Just you and me, Mr. Luke?" I gasp, looking around me.

"And me," says Rev, smiling. "It's a long trip and Luke needs somebody to help with the driving."

"Can I go, Daddy?" asks Trace, excitement in his eyes. "I want to see a Negro League baseball game!"

"Yes, son. Seeing how good these colored players are will change the way you see baseball; change the way you see life."

"And Mason's going, too," says Rev. "That's why you're here, son," he adds, turning to Mason.

Mason's mouth drops open. He stares at me in disbelief. Then his face lights up in the biggest grin I've ever seen from him. "Wow! Thanks, Rev!"

"Hey, I want to go," says Hope, frowning.

Gran gives Hope's arm a squeeze. "Baby, it's just men on this trip. You and I can go another time." Hope's shoulders slump, and her eyes get shiny.

Rev walks over and kisses Hope on the top of her head. "Don't be sad, sweetie. We'll bring back something real special for you."

"Hey! We've got something special for you now," says Mason. "Come on, Cato."

Puzzled, I walk behind Mason as he goes over to the station wagon and opens the back door.

"Got a present for Hope." He pulls the box from the middle seat and hands it to me. "But you should give it to her."

His eyes widen impatiently. He looks back and forth between the box and Hope, like I'm supposed to know what he's talking about. And suddenly, I do. Can't help but smile.

When I turn around, though, I have a somber look on my face. I walk over to Hope. "Guess what I've got."

"How should I know?" barks Hope, tears now streaming down her face from disappointment.

"Well, pull the blanket back and see."

Hope scrunches up her nose, wipes her face with both hands, and rolls her eyes. She reaches into the box and pulls back a corner of the blanket. Moses's golden head pops up. He opens his mouth to yawn, then lets out a loud *meow.*

"*Moses!* Oh. My. Goodness! Moses!" Hope rips the blanket off the kitten and takes him up in her arms. "Moses, you've come home to me!"

"What in the world?" Rev takes off his cap and scratches his head.

"Long story," I say, looking at Mason.

"Maybe I won't miss going to Kansas City so much now," says Hope. "Moses needs me!"

We hear another loud purr from Moses as Hope cradles him in her arms.

"We'll go to Kansas City again next summer, Hope, when you and Gran and Papa Vee can come too," says Mr. Luke, but Hope's not listening anymore.

Me and Trace and Mason look at one another. "Kansas City!" we shout at the same time, jumping up in the air and slapping hands.

Rev smiles and shakes his head. "Let's eat, people! Mo's spirit is waiting for us to polish off the fried chicken, greens, and cornbread and get to his favorite dessert. Come on!"

Rev puts his arm around Gran and pulls her into the house. The rest of us follow.

We sit down at the kitchen table, Papa Vee at the head on one end and Rev on the other. Gran and Hope have laid out the food for Daddy Mo's birthday dinner just like Sunday supper. Fried chicken, collard greens, cornbread muffins, and candied yams. While we're eating, Rev does most of the talking, telling us all how exciting it is to see the Monarchs play the Homestead Grays, a fantastic team out of Pittsburgh.

Mr. Luke clears his throat. "Well, you haven't lived until you've been to Chicago to see the Negro Leagues' East-West All-Star Game. I was there three years ago. Me and fifteen or twenty thousand other people."

Isaac shakes his head and laughs. "The newspaper said that last year there were fifty thousand people at the game in Chicago, Mr. Luke."

"*Fifty thousand people?*" yells Mr. Luke.

"White and colored together, you know," says Philly Dan.

"Well, I'll be! That's more than go to all-star games for Major League Baseball."

Rev clears his throat. "Uh, Mama J? Where *is* that big ole chocolate cake you cook every year for Mo's birthday? My mouth is watering for it."

Gran sits the prettiest cake I have ever seen on the center of the table. This year, it's three layers high, covered in chocolate icing with pecan halves arranged in a circle on top and strewn around the sides. Bet my mouth is watering more than Rev's.

"Okay, Mama J, Papa Vee gets the first slice and I get the second," announces Rev, watching every move of the knife as Gran slices the chocolate cake.

"Amos Whitfield!" Gran stops to look at her adopted son. "Where are your manners? Company gets to eat cake before you."

"Due respect, Mama J, but Moses was the only brother I ever had. When we honor him, the only person I take a back seat to is Papa Vee."

No one says a word.

"Oh. And you, Mama J."

Papa Vee shakes his head. "Pass me a piece of cake and give the next one to Amos so he can shut up and eat. Don't make me take you out to the woodshed, son."

Everybody laughs.

"Thank you kindly, Mama J." Rev lifts his plate off the table, brings it up close to his face, and shoves a huge piece of chocolate cake into his mouth. "Hmm," he mumbles as the rest of us wait to get our serving.

When his plate is finally empty, Rev puts his fork down and starts in on a story.

"Now I know you won't believe this, but Mo liked chocolate cake even when he was a baby with nary a tooth in his mouth."

Having never heard this story before, Trace and Mason and Philly Dan look at Rev, puzzled—wondering, no doubt, why such a whopper would come out of a preacher's mouth.

Mr. Luke drops his head and laughs into his hand. Me and Isaac and Hope just shake our heads. We've heard this story many times before, and we love it every time. Truth be told, it's more like a fairy tale. Rev didn't know Daddy Mo as a baby. When he came to live here, Daddy Mo was ten.

Now Rev is waving his arms in the air, acting out the funniest parts of the story. Everybody is laughing, even Papa Vee. I look around the table at my family, at my friends. Isaac is sitting right across from me. And…

Clear as day, I see two figures standing on either side of him, Daddy Mo on his left and Satchel Paige on his right. They're both staring at me, the corners of their mouths turned up in a smile. Each one gives me a thumbs-up sign, and my face breaks out in a big grin.

I know what this sign means.

I'll be pitching for the Kansas City Monarchs someday, just like my brother and my father before him. And maybe, just maybe, Satchel Paige will teach me how to pitch as good as him.


WARRIOR ON THE MOUND
Back pages:
Author's Note
History in the News!
Real Baseball Players the Pender County Rangers are Named For
Timeline of Black Americans in Baseball
Works that Inspired the Writing of *Warrior on the Mound*
More Middle Grade Historical Baseball Novels

# AUTHOR'S NOTE

*Warrior on the Mound* is not a true story, but the setting is real and some of the characters are based on real people who lived a long time ago. The Pender County Rangers and the New Hanover Marlins were wholly invented, but their story is grounded in historical facts.

The Negro National League was formed in 1920 by Rube Foster because Black players were barred from Major League Baseball teams from the 1800s when the "Gentleman's Agreement" was put in force by team owners until 1947 when Jackie Robinson joined the Brooklyn Dodgers. The main character, Cato Jones, was named for Octavius Valentine Catto, an amateur baseball player, high school teacher, and social activist who lived in Philadelphia from the 1840s to the 1870s. During this period, Black players were not allowed to join Major League Baseball teams. Catto, a second baseman for the Philadelphia Pythians, succeeded in challenging white teams to play against them in interracial baseball games.

# HISTORY IN THE NEWS!

The events in *Warrior on the Mound* take place in the 1930s, but they are built on historical events that can be traced to the 1800s. In an extraordinary coincidence, several themes that were highlighted in *Warrior on the Mound* generated notable contemporary news in 2020, 2021, and 2022.

In 2020, the centennial of the founding of the Negro National League in 1920 by Rube Foster, Major League Baseball (MLB) formally recognized teams and players from the Negro Leagues as part of professional baseball. It means that the performances of players in the Negro Leagues will be folded into baseball statistics and these players will get credit for the records that they set. Finally!

The setting for *Warrior on the Mound* is near the city of Wilmington, North Carolina. An event that happened there over a century ago became timely again with the republication of a book about the events of 1898, which were incorrectly called a race riot. A report commissioned by the state of North Carolina in 2006 revealed that the event was actually an insurrection and not a riot. In 1898, a coalition of Black and white citizens, former members of the Republican and Fusion parties, were elected to citywide offices. They were overthrown and forced out of town by armed vigilantes called Red Shirts who identified with the Democratic party. From the official report documenting the event, a book was published in 2009, then revised and reissued in 2020 (Umfleet, Lerae Sikes. *A Day of Blood: The 1898 Wilmington Race Riot*. Chapel Hill, North Carolina: The University of North Carolina Press, 2020). A second book about these events won the 2021 Pulitzer Prize (Zucchino, David. *Wilmington's Lie. The Murderous Coup of 1898 and the Rise of White Supremacy*. New York, New York: Grove Atlantic, Inc., 2020).

# THE PENDER COUNTY RANGERS ARE NAMED FOR REAL BASEBALL PLAYERS

To honor Black baseball players, the Pender County Rangers characters in this book were named after players from Negro League baseball. Their ball field was named for a Black player from the 1800s.

*The Rangers home field, Walker Field*, was named for *Moses Fleetwood Walker*, who played one season as catcher in 1883 with the Toledo Blue Stockings of the American Association of Professional Baseball, a major league organization. He then played on various minor league teams until 1889 and was the last Black player to participate at the major league level until Jackie Robinson joined the Brooklyn Dodgers in 1947.

*Hank, right fielder*, is named for *Henry Louis "Hank" Aaron,* who played for the Indianapolis Clowns (Negro American League). He also played 23 seasons in Major League Baseball with the Milwaukee and Atlanta Braves (National League) and the Milwaukee Brewers (American League). Aaron broke the career home-run record set by Babe Ruth. He was inducted into the National Baseball Hall of Fame in 1982.

*Raymond D., third baseman*, was named for *Raymond Emmett Dandridge*, who played for the Newark Eagles of the Negro National League from 1936 to 1939 and in 1942 and 1944. He played for many other Negro League teams. Dandridge was inducted into the National Baseball Hall of Fame in 1987.

*CP, center fielder,* was named for *James Thomas "Cool Papa" Bell*, called the fastest man in baseball. He played for the following Negro League teams: the Saint Louis Stars, the Kansas City Monarchs, the Pittsburgh Crawfords, and the Homestead Grays. He was inducted into the National Baseball Hall of Fame in 1974.

*Smokey Joe, relief pitcher,* is named for *Joseph "Smokey Joe" Williams*. He played most of his 27 years pitching for the Homestead Grays. Williams was inducted into the National Baseball Hall of Fame in 1999.

*Monte, left field*, is named for *Monte Irvin*, who played for the Newark Eagles of the Negro National League. He also played for the major league teams the New York Giants and the Chicago Cubs. Irvin was inducted into the National Baseball Hall of Fame in 1973.

———

## TIMELINE OF BLACK AMERICANS IN BASEBALL

### 1872–1889
Bud Fowler and Moses Fleetwood Walker were among the first Black Americans to play on all-white baseball teams in both the major and minor leagues.

### 1887–88
The "Gentleman's Agreement" was adopted. It was an informal pact among owners of major league teams that banned Black players from their teams. The "agreement" remained in place for 60 years, until Jackie Robinson joined the Brooklyn Dodgers in 1947.

### 1920
Negro League baseball was launched by Rube Foster, owner of the Chicago American Giants, who organized eight teams into the Negro National Baseball League. A few years later, white owners of Black teams formed the Eastern Colored League. The best team in each of these leagues played in the Colored World Series, which started in 1924 with a matchup between the Kansas City Monarchs and Hilldale Athletic Club. The Monarchs won.

### 1920–1962
The Kansas City Monarchs were the longest running franchise in Negro League baseball. They were part of the Negro National League from

1920 to 1930, the year of that league's demise. From 1930 until 1962, the Monarchs were part of the Negro American League. The Monarchs were formed from J. L. Wilkinson's multiracial All-Nations team and players from the Twenty-Fifth Infantry Wreckers, an all-Black team. Their name can be traced to the Monarch Printing Company in Kansas City and was derived from the Monarch butterfly.

## 1930
The Kansas City Monarchs of the Negro National League were the first team in America to have night games using a portable lighting system. Major League Baseball teams did not have lights that allowed them to play night games until 1935.

## 1933–1962
In 1933, Gus Greenlee, owner of the Pittsburgh Crawfords, was inspired to create the first East-West All-Star Classic at Comiskey Park in Chicago. Players were nominated by fans, and votes were tallied by two prominent Black newspapers, the *Chicago Defender* and the *Pittsburgh Courier.* Attendance at the game was sometimes as high as 20,000 to 50,000 fans, much larger than crowds for most MLB all-star games.

## 1946–1947
Jackie Robinson became the first Black player to play on a Major League Baseball team since the 1880s. He joined the Brooklyn Dodgers of the National League. Larry Doby was the first Black player to join an American League team, the Cleveland Indians.

# WORKS THAT INSPIRED THE WRITING
## OF *WARRIOR ON THE MOUND*

Nelson, Kadir. *We are the Ship: The Story of Negro League Baseball*. New York: Jump at the Sun/Hyperion Books for Children, an imprint of Disney Book Group, 2008. This author-illustrated picture book is an excellent reference to the history of Negro League baseball with stunningly beautiful paintings of individual players and historical games such as the East-West All-Star Classic at Comiskey Field in Chicago and the 1924 Negro World Series.

Gratz, Alan. *Brooklyn Nine: A Novel in Nine Innings*. New York: Dial Books, A member of Penguin Group (USA), Inc., 2009. This book is a series of novellas about the Schneider-Flint family and their love of baseball, from the first immigrants who came to America to the fans who suffered the departure of the Dodgers from Brooklyn to Los Angeles.

Gratz, Alan. *Samurai Shortstop*. New York: Dial Books for Young Readers, 2006. In this novel, set in 1890 Tokyo, Japan, a young Samurai in training learns that his new skills help him to become an exceptional baseball player.

Hughes, Langston. *The Weary Blues*. New York: Alfred A. Knopf, 1926. This was the first of many books of poetry published by the revered poet and writer whose work mirrored the challenges faced by African Americans in the early and mid-twentieth century.

Park, Linda Sue. *Keeping Score*. New York: Clarion Books, 2008. In this novel, a young girl roots for the New York Giants to win against the New York Yankees in the memorable 1951 World Series.

Tooke, Wes. *King of the Mound: My Summer with Satchel Paige*. New York: Simon and Schuster Books for Young Readers, 2013. In this novel, a young pitcher recovering from a bout with polio meets the great Negro League pitcher Satchel Paige and is inspired to overcome his personal setbacks to achieve his goal to pitch again.

Burns, Ken, Lynn Novick, Geoffrey C. Ward, and John Chancellor. *Baseball*. Hollywood, California: PBS Distribution, 2010.

Burns, Ken, Lynn Novick, Geoffrey C. Ward, and John Chancellor. *The Tenth Inning*. Hollywood, California: PBS Distribution, 2010. These series of films by Ken Burns and company are a definitive history of the greatest American pastime by the most distinguished documentarian of the twentieth and twenty-first centuries.

---

## MORE HISTORICAL MIDDLE GRADE BASEBALL NOVELS

Weinstein, Barry. *Waiting for Pumpsie*. Watertown, MA: Charlesbridge, 2017.

Robinson, Sharon. *The Hero Two Doors Down*. New York: Scholastic, Inc, 2016.

Fishman, Cathy Goldberg. *When Jackie and Hank Met*. New York: Marshall Cavendish Children's Books, a subsidiary of Times Publishing Group, 2012.

Myers, Walter Dean. *My Name Is America: The Journal of Biddy Owens, Birmingham, Alabama, 1948*. New York: Scholastic Paperbacks, 2001.

Gutman, Dan. *Jackie and Me*. New York: HarperCollins, 2000.

Gutman, Dan. *Satchel and Me*. New York: Amistad, an imprint of HarperCollins, Inc., 2009.

Hubbard, Crystal. *Catching the Moon: The Story of a Young Girl's Baseball Dream*. New York: Lee & Low Books, 2010.

Rappaport, Doreen and Lyndall, Callan. *Dirt on Their Skirts: The Story of the Young Women Who Won the World Championship*. New York: Penguin Putnam, Inc./Dial Books for Young Readers, 2000.

Mochizuki, Ken. *Baseball Saved Us*. New York: Lee and Low Books, 1995.